MISS ADVENTURE #1

Tangle in Tijuana

Lilla and Nora Zuckerman

A FIRESIDE BOOK
Published by Simon & Schuster
New York · London · Toronto · Sydney · Singapore

FIRESIDE
Rockefeller Center
1230 Avenue of the Americas
New York, NY 10020

FIRESIDE and colophon are registered
trademarks of Simon & Schuster, Inc.

For information about special discounts for bulk purchases,
please contact Simon & Schuster Special Sales:
1-800-456-6798 or business@simonandschuster.com

DESIGNED BY LAUREN SIMONETTI

Manufactured in the United States of America

1 3 5 7 9 10 8 6 4 2

Library of Congress Cataloging-in-Publication Data
Zuckerman, Lilla.
Tangle in Tijuana / Lilla and Nora Zuckerman.
    p.   cm.—(Miss Adventures ; bk. 1)
1. Tijuana (Baja California, Mexico)—Fiction. I. Zuckerman, Nora. II. Title.
PS3626.U27 T3 2003
813'.6—dc21
2002030404
ISBN 0-7432-3845-1

Stop right there! Read this first!

This is a *Miss Adventure!* Meaning it's interactive—not one of those stodgy old books where you start reading on the first page and finish on the last. At the end of every chapter you will be asked to make a decision and flip to the corresponding page. You're in the driver's seat, so think carefully—your decisions may make the difference between finding Mr. Right, or finding yourself in a Tijuana prison.

This is your *Miss Adventure,* so have a ball—and **no cheating!** True Miss Adventurers roll with the punches and never look back. Have fun, don't drink the water, and we'll see you south of the border.

MISS ADVENTURE #1

Tangle
in
Tijuana

You are hurtling down the freeway toward the Mexican border, hanging your head out of the window in an attempt to gasp some fresh air to cure your wicked hangover. But the glaring Southern California sunshine and the grumbling of the V-8 engine are only making your headache worse. Last night you made a drunken promise to your best friend, Lani, that you would go with her on her annual trip to Tijuana. Little did you know, she was actually serious. Now you find yourself riding shotgun in Lani's beat up 1970's Mustang, wearing your new Betsey Johnson sundress and the biggest shades you could find. In your hangover haze you figured that if you are going on a Mexican vacation, you might as well do it in style. Looking over at Lani behind the wheel, smoking a cigarette and drinking her third Diet Coke of the morning, you wonder what you've gotten yourself into. You've never been to Tijuana, but it seems like everybody has a story about their bizarre experiences south of the border, and you kind of want one too.

"This is absolutely the best medicine for you," Lani says with conviction. She drags on a menthol cigarette and passes it to you. "Nothing perks you up quite like Diet Cokes and menthol cigarettes in the morning."

"I don't know if this is the best idea," you say, not wanting to hurt her feelings. "I just bought these sandals a week ago and I've heard that Tijuana is not really an open-toe-shoe kind of town."

"Hello! This is the modern world," Lani exclaims. "It's not all burro shit and tapeworms. Tijuana is actually the most-visited foreign city by Americans. It's practically Disneyland, with a shitload of booze, but no scary cartoon creatures. At least, I think there aren't any scary cartoon creatures. I used to go there all the time when I was a teenager. The clubs actually accepted my junior high school ID."

"How come every story I have ever heard about TJ has involved a Mexican prison, donkey shows, and a case of ungodly food poisoning?"

"As long as you don't urinate in public or start a knife fight you are not going to jail. You are forgetting that TJ is a magical place where you can toss a rock in the air and hit a hottie. Everybody goes there to hook up, it's like a never-ending bachelor party."

"Okay, but I don't want to just drink and make out with boys named Pedro—I am bringing some good shit home," you say. You've always been a shopper at heart, and have heard there are lots of special knickknacks you can buy in Mexico: prescription drugs, fireworks, endangered species . . . all at bargain prices.

"Oh shit—fleeing family!" Lani points to a massive yellow road sign with a silhouette of a family dashing across the high-way. It reminds you of "deer crossing" signs you've seen. "This means we're close. Beware of fleeing families!"

"Yeah, bitches! You makin' a run for the border?"

An obnoxious SUV full of drunken fratboys have pulled up alongside Lani's car. They are wielding a video camera and hanging out of the sunroof. One of them sticks his tongue out and makes an obscene gesture you have not seen since sum-mer camp.

"Ah, the modern mating call," you sigh.

Lani gives them the finger. "Eat me!" she yells across the

highway, laying on her horn. She turns to you with a grin. "Hell yeah. We are going to have the *best* time."

Lani lets you finish the menthol cigarette as the highway signs begin to get bigger and more exciting: "Last Exit to USA," "Border Crossing Ahead," "U-turn to USA." Tijuana is moments away.

"Alright—here's the deal. We can park on the American side of the border and walk across or we can park over in Mexico," Lani explains. "If we pull over and park here, it's a little pricey, and it's a walk, but the car is definitely safer. And you know I love this car."

"I'm wearing open-toe Prada sandals and just got a pedicure," you say. "Just a note."

"Or, if we park over there, we can be close to the car, drop shit off occasionally, and smuggle large items across the border—in case you were thinking about investing in anything—you know, heavy artillery, bobcats," Lani continues, "but the car might get jacked and we should probably kiss the hubcaps good-bye right now."

You toss the menthol out the window and scrounge around in your purse for some Visine. "Fuck—I'm too hungover to think straight," you sigh, as you glance down at your strappy shoes.

"You decide, princess," Lani grins "'cause I can smell Mexico already!"

If you park in the U.S. and decide to hoof it over the border, turn to page 6.

If you motor across and take your chances, turn to page 8.

Although it's always nice to have your own car, your own music selections, and your own ashtray, you can't really imagine that Lani's car would leave Mexico intact.

Lani pulls into a huge parking lot, where for a simple three-dollar fee, you get your very own parking spot and peace of mind. They even seem to speak English here!

The two of you follow the crowd heading for the border. *Bienvenido!* Welcome to Mexico! Just about everywhere you look there's a smiling welcome sign. You navigate your way through tourist families and drunken bachelor parties, finally reaching the border crossing. It's like Checkpoint Charlie, only with kids running around. You cross a bridge above the long line of cars waiting to be let into Mexico. Looming ahead is an elaborate turnstile. One turn and whoosh—you're in Tijuana. A long line of cabs waits for girls just like you. You and Lani pick one with air conditioning.

"Take us to the center of town!" you bark at the driver, excitedly.

"*El centro!*" Lani shouts, like she's drunk already. The taxi sputters onto a highway and you're immediately sitting in traffic.

"So, what's there to do around here?" you ask the driver. He replies in broken English.

"There is lots to shop for. You know, tequila, sombrero, purses for the ladies . . ."

"We're gonna hit some clubs," Lani explains.

"Oh. Yeeeah. Lots of discos for the ladies. I know number-one club in town, they treat you very nice."

It's still a little early to go to a dance club, but looking around you figure Tijuana must be kind of like Vegas—a twenty-four-hour town. As the cab creeps along, you hear pounding music from every club. They all have cheesy themes, lots of galvanized metal and neon. Très 1980s. You drive past one place that even has a communist theme and a beach volleyball court on the roof. You wonder if the commies know they've gone *Baywatch*.

"Lani," you ask, "Would it be considered unladylike to do the Electric Slide before you've had lunch?"

"Fuck ladylike," Lani says, rolling down the window and hocking a loogie. "We're here for boozin' and cruisin' south of the border. This isn't Taco Bell, this is the real shit."

"But do we need to hear 'Mambo Number Five' right away? We could do some shopping first, then hit the dance floor."

Lani lowers her voice. "He said he knows number-one club in town. They treat us very *nice*."

"Where we go?" your driver asks. "I have to turn up here. *Vámonos.*"

If you can't stomach the dance club so early, hit the marketplace and do some shopping by turning to page 11.

When you're at the swimming pool, you gotta go off the high dive, right? Go clubbing and turn to page 19.

Tangle in Tijuana

You have decided that you would rather put Lani's car at risk than walk around all day. Besides, you never know when you're going to need a quick getaway . . .

You are surprised how easy it is to just drive across the border into a foreign country. One would think they would be worried. Hell, you could be carrying secret-weapons plans or something. You mention this to Lani and she just laughs.

"Dude, getting into Mexico is easy. It's leaving that's a bitch. Border guards know that American dollars can buy anything your heart desires. Where do you think I get that kind bud?"

"Bienvenidos a México!" reads the red, white, and green sign that hangs over the multiple lanes of cars and trucks. Suddenly, you're in a sea of humanity. You feel like you're driving into the world's largest swap meet. Vendors swarm around the cars, trying to sell all things cheap and colorful. Lanyards, ceramic monkeys, sombreros, even those ponchos you thought went out of style with Jams in the 1980s. There was an older surfer boy you liked who used to wear one every day that smelled faintly of marijuana and sea salt. Not surprisingly, that is exactly what Tijuana smells like.

"Hey! Stop daydreaming and roll up the window!" Lani screams, "If you don't, somebody's gonna grab your hair, chop it off, and sell it! It happened to my cousin's friend's sister, I *swear*."

Lani quickly steers the car toward the highway exit. All the other cars are traveling in a pack together, but Lani was never one to do that type of thing.

"Shouldn't we just follow everyone else?"

"No way. I know a great place to park, and it's totally free."

Lani pulls her car into the worst neighborhood you have ever seen in your whole entire life. And you have been to Detroit. She has to slam on her brakes at one point to avoid a roaming pack of dogs carrying what must have once been a chicken. You are beginning to get the feeling that it has been a long time since Lani has been to Tijuana.

"Check this out! Parking gods have smiled upon us!" Lani pulls her car into a patch of dirt near a rickety shack.

"Uh, I think you just parked in somebody's front yard," you say.

"If this was a yard, it would have grass," Lani says. You want to protest, but she just seems so excited about the whole thing. "Have another cigarette and chill the fuck out. I know what I'm doing, this is prime real estate."

You look around the car for anything you might need in the future. Even the little evergreen-tree freshener seems to look at you and say "don't leave me here all alone, I'm frightened."

You and Lani find that you are really not that far from the center of town. A few quick blocks and you are in the middle of a huge marketplace square. It's overwhelming, people are everywhere.

"So what should we do first?" you ask Lani. It's early and you have the whole day in front of you.

"Breakfast margaritas are always an option," she says with a devilish glint in her eye. "That will knock your hangover the fuck out. Or we can use this sober time to go shopping. You can pick up some supplies, if you know what I mean."

Though you don't really know what she means, you nod like you do.

If you decide that drinking before lunch is not a great idea but that shopping always is, turn to page 13.

If you think that nothing cures a hangover like more booze, perhaps a breakfast margarita is the morning pick-me-up you never knew you needed, turn to page 16.

You decide to follow your mantra, "I Shop, Therefore I Am."

"Drop us off at the marketplace," you tell the driver.

He lets you off at a huge plaza packed with shops and tourists. It's like a cheap mall, only here everything's either stolen or made out of straw. Purses, jackets, those Spicoli stoner ponchos, sombreros, bullwhips, belts, fake flowers, piñatas shaped as Pokémon . . . this place has everything you never knew you wanted.

"I feel this irresistible need for fake silver jewelry and Selena memorial T-shirts," Lani sighs.

"You can get all that and so much more for a mere five dollars."

"Ladies, start your engines," Lani shouts, startling the others around you. She has the fever. You're both about to descend and spend when . . . *boom!* You're literally surrounded by a mob of children.

"Gum? Chicklet?" they plead. All of them are selling boxes of Chicklets, gum in every flavor and color. You never knew there was such a market. And so many kids, all of them looking at you with their beautiful, soulful eyes.

"They think we have money," Lani whispers to you.

"That's because we *do*," you whisper back. The kids are adorable and friendly. All they want is for you to buy some gum; it will make their lives so much better. You find your hand reaching for your wallet.

"You're not gonna buy gum, are you?" Lani says, disappointed. "You're so weak. The gum sucks. It's like Nicorette without the nicotine."

In the back of your mind, some residual memory of Sally Struthers pleads at you from the television. She's crying for you to "Think of the children!" Five dollars is five dollars, it means nothing to you and everything to them. But, this could also be some sort of scam. There could be a mugger waiting to come at you from the shadows the second you take out your wallet. Kids are just kids, but kids today can be brutal. And if kids are brutal, then Tijuana kids might be downright vicious.

Drop a fiver and make some kid's day. Nobody can have enough good karma. To chew all day, turn to page 135.

Actually, you find this disturbing. Little cute kids sent out to manipulate you out of your money? Tell the kids to vamoose and turn to page 188.

You have decided to forego the margarita madness until lunchtime—besides, who could resist the allure of a Tijuana shopping spree?

The ingenuity of the Mexican locals never ceases to amaze you. There are no beggars in Mexico, only vendors. Everyone has something to sell. You cannot believe the multitude of crappy wares made from crappy products being sold in what seems like the world's largest garage sale. As you and Lani puff on menthols, you try to respectfully peruse such little treasures as cross-shaped necklaces made out of yarn, and adobe piggybanks shaped like that creepy purple dinosaur Barney.

"Do people really buy this junk?" you ask.

"Wait till you've had a couple shots of tequila in your system," Lani answers, "you won't get out of this damned country without at least one 'Life's a Beach' Corona T-shirt. Sad but true." You vaguely remember Lani wearing one to the gym once or twice . . .

You continue to cruise around the enormous swap-meet, chain smoking so that you can wield the lit cigarette as a weapon, fending off gypsy children and the young male locals—who can't help but notice two foxy American ladies. Lani seriously considers buying a vase that looks like a giant penis, while you weigh the options of owning a purse that looks like a coconut.

You are gazing at a stand of Mexican cigars and X-rated playing cards when a thin, fast-talking vendor starts grinning wildly at you and asks, "You girls want to see what's behind the counter?"

"Sure, señor," Lani replies easily. She gives you a little "what the hell?" kind of shrug. You assume she knows what she's doing, and try to act cool.

The man leads you to the back of his stand, takes a patterned blanket off of a trunk, and flips it open. Inside, the trunk is filled to capacity with sticks of dynamite.

"What in the hell is that?" you ask, "Anti-aircraft?"

"No lady—it's for Cinco de Mayo—how you say?" the man chatters, "Fourth of July—no?"

"Fireworks," Lani grins, "can't get this shit west of the Rocky Mountains—you would have to road trip out to Missouri or somewhere like that."

"No, no, no," the man continues, "cannot buy in America."

"What the hell would we do with explosives?" you ask.

"Do you know what my little brother and his pyromaniac friends would pay for this stuff?" she asks.

"Hell," you reply, "Do you know how much *our* pyromaniac friends would pay for this stuff? We'd be too cool for school."

You think back to your younger days when entertainment was made more simply, with an aerosol hairspray can and a lighter. The fireworks *could* come in handy—they would make one hell of a party favor. You momentarily consider torching all of your ex-boyfriend memorabilia in one fiery flash.

On the other hand, do you really want to cart around explosives all day? What if you're drunk, and try to light a cigarette and—it's too horrible to think about. And what about getting this shit past the border? Do they really lock up nice American girls for tiny transgressions like smuggling explosives? I mean, you saw *Brokedown Palace*.

"Well cowgirl," Lani chuckles, "what do you think?"

If you decide to start a small international arms trade for the sheer hell of it, buy the fireworks and turn to page 90.

If you conclude that you are not to be trusted with highly combustible materials at this fragile, emotional time, walk on and turn to page 28.

Anytime is party time in Mexico, right? You have decided to strap one on early and get this fiesta rolling!

"I know this killer place where the margaritas are as perfect as they come," Lani raves as you walk through the dusty down-town streets. "I have done extensive field research, and these are going to be the best damn fruity drinks you've ever had." She turns to you and whispers, "They *import* American tap water to make their own ice." You try to act impressed.

Around a corner you are suddenly mobbed on the street by dozens of young men shoving flyers in your face. You feel like you are in a swarm of bees.

"Two for one Coronas!"

"Buy one Corona, get two margaritas free!"

"Free tequila for pretty ladies!"

"Buy one margarita, get a free taco!"

You think about that really depressing movie where the guy goes to Vegas to drink himself to death and wonder if Tijuana would have been a more appropriate choice. Lani grabs your hand and shuffles you out of the fray.

"Aahh—here we are," she announces.

You glance up at a two-level bar that seems to be decorated exclusively with piñatas and beer signage. "Mamacita's" is painted over the door, directly under a balcony that looks like it could crumble at any moment, crushing the dozens of drunken teens below.

The second you walk through the door, an air-raid-like siren sounds, scaring the living shit out of you. Lights flash wildly.

Two large men approach you, and swing you over their shoulders. Suddenly you are upside down, spinning around and then finally deposited at a large booth. Before you can blink, two frozen margaritas are in front of your face.

"I didn't order this," you manage to say, your shock only now subsiding.

"It's like one of those fancy restaurants where they decide what you should have *for* you," Lani answers, between healthy chugs of marg.

You begin to down your margarita—you have to admit, it's damn good. You both light up, and before you exhale, four Coronas are on the table.

"Free with the drink," Lani explains.

About four margaritas and countless freebies later, you're really beginning to dig the whole country of Mexico. You don't even mind "Who Let the Dogs Out," which has been played about a dozen times. Just as Lani is teaching you to say "suck my cock" in Spanish, your waiter approaches.

"Compliments of Mamacita's," he says, laying down two shot glasses in front of you. "House specialty."

He pours Lani a tequila shot and she downs it like a pro. It's your turn. He pours your shot and—*plunk!*—something falls into the glass! "Ahhhhhh!!!" shrieks Lani, "The Worm!" The air-raid siren goes off again, lights blare, the music screeches to a halt, and all eyes are on you.

"What on god's green earth is that?" you ask, as you stare into the shot glass. Floating in your glass is a small, white, emaciated little clump of flesh that had been sitting at the bottom of that bottle for who knows how long.

"The worm," your waiter explains, "is very good luck—an

aphrodisiac—you must drink it down all at once and you are guaranteed good fortune!"

"You're shitting me," you say. "It's a goddamn earthworm and I wouldn't eat it if I were on an island competing for a million dollars."

"Dude!" exclaims Lani, "You have to do it—it's a once-in-a-lifetime thing! You might disgrace the bartender if you don't. And you will have the *best* story and bragging rights for years."

"*Drink!*"

"*Drink!*"

"*Drink!*"

The bar has exploded in chants and cheers. You get a huge adrenaline rush from the chanting crowd and know it's now or never. You *are* pretty loaded—you could drink petrol and it wouldn't faze you. You pick up the glass, your slimy little friend floating inside . . .

"*Eat the worm!*"

"*Eat the worm!*"

If you decide to throw all sense and reason out the door (and isn't that why you are in Mexico?), throw that little sucker down the gullet and turn to page 185.

You cannot muster the strength or will to actually eat the worm. Who cares if you disgrace the bar? It is disgraceful to serve you, a paying customer, a worm. Put down the glass and turn to page 93.

To quote the movie **Cocktail**, *"Beer is for breakfast. Drink or be gone." You always did like that line, time to live it. You are having a liquid brunch!*

"To the club!" you scream to the taxi driver. Lani sticks her head out the window and yells *"Arriba! Arriba!"* As the driver turns onto another street, you have to grab Lani by the belt to keep her from falling out the window. You yank her back down to the seat.

"Easy there, señorita," you say.

"Fuck easy. Somewhere in this town there are about six margaritas with my name on them . . . I can taste them already." She starts applying body glitter to her cheeks and shoulders. In Lani's world, it's never too early for glitter. The cab screeches to a halt and you toss the cabbie a fiver. The club you've arrived at looks like a converted factory, tricked out with wildly colored pipes and sheet metal. The sign reads "El Machine."

"Hmm, just what I wanted," you say to Lani outside the club, "a bar that celebrates industrial sprawl."

"I'll tell you one thing," she says, entering the club, "El Machine better be the kind of machine that pours stiff drinks." You strut into the cavernous club. There are three circular levels of balconies that look down onto a giant rotating dance floor. Whoever started this club probably didn't have to apply for pesky business licenses and health inspections, so instead they blew their wad on lasers, smoke machines, and strobe lights.

"I need a drink, *stat!*" you scream in Lani's ear. She grabs you by the wrist and you weave your way through the booths and tables, instantly feeling like a piece of meat. You lose count of how many times your ass gets grabbed by anonymous men. One table of guys gives you a thumbs up and yells "Eight and a half!" Another greasy fellow brushes by you and says you are "prime orgy material." Trying to take this all as a compliment is proving difficult. You have only been here forty-five seconds and feel like you've just run the sexual harassment gauntlet.

Finally you reach the bar. It shines in neon splendor, and you welcome it like a sailor welcomes a lighthouse after crossing stormy seas. You and Lani light cigarettes and inhale deeply. "Lani," you sigh with relief, "I feel violated. Like, nude-photos-on-the-internet violated."

"Hey! Hey! Thirsty ladies here!" Lani yells to the bartender. He looks up and gives you a sign to hold on for a minute. You look down to see he is in the middle of preparing about six margaritas the size of paint buckets. Make no mistake, these drinks are bigger than your torso and each elaborate glass has a plastic shark or surfer hanging out the top. A really handsome guy pays for the booze, peeling bills off a huge roll.

"Could you help me with something?" he asks, smiling at you. He has blindingly perfect white teeth. You always were a sucker for good dental hygiene.

"Help you?" you say in your best sexy voice, "I don't work for tips, flyboy." Damn, you are good.

"Well, do you work for obnoxiously large alcoholic beverages?" he asks.

Lani, who has just overheard the magic words, pops her

head over your shoulder and tells the white-teeth man, "Interesting. Go on."

"I'm sitting over there with a few friends and could use some help carrying these drinks. You can have what you can carry." You glance over to where he indicates his friends are sitting. They are nowhere near the ass-grabbing-gauntlet, thank God. In fact, they seem like five clean-cut guys with their own minibar. Their table is loaded with bottles of vodka, tequila, pitchers of juices, and shit, is that sangria?

"What do you think?" you whisper to Lani.

"Up to you," she answers, "but do we really want to get comfortable now? We haven't even done a lap." True, you have yet to see what else the three layers of club has to offer in the way of men, but judging from your recent trauma of being called "prime orgy material," do you really want to know?

Carrying drinks is one of your favorite exercises, and your second favorite is drinking copious amounts of booze with handsome men. Turn to page 173.

When you're shopping for shoes, do you buy the first pair you try on? I think not. Tell the toothy guy good-bye and shop around a little. Turn to page 64.

You just saw one of those local news exposés about how unsanitary restaurants are. In Mexico, it can only be worse. After careful consideration, you've decided that it is better to see your food made in front of you.

"One taco," you say, trying not to make it sound like the word "taco" has a question mark behind it. The grilling bandito takes a long hit off his spliff and smiles through graying teeth. You wonder momentarily if the tacos are responsible for his stripped tooth enamel.

"Cheecken or meeet?"

"Don't you mean chicken or *beef*?"

"Cheecken or meeet?"

Lani shoots you a look of warning.

"Cheek . . . Chicken."

The Taco Bandito turns around and takes some raw chicken from a plastic container. Whew. At least this guy has plastic. It's not like he keeps his meat in a bag woven from natural fibers.

"You like spicy?"

You shrug noncommittally and the Taco Bandito opens up his grease-stained shirt, revealing a bandoleer of spices and peppers. This guy probably wakes up every morning and straps it on like he's going to war. Tijuana does sort of have a battlefield quality to it.

"On second thought, go light on the spicy," you say, trying to smile.

"Light spicy," he says, and then proceeds to toss your chicken with various pinches of spices from his bandoleer.

"It's for flavor," Lani whispers in awe.

You watch the Taco Bandito as he tosses the chicken around on the grill like he's been doing it for years, spiking the meat with cilantro and onions. Your mouth begins to water as the smell hits you.

"This is going to be the best taco *ever*," you whisper, hypnotized by the sizzle of the meat. The flour tortilla goes on the grill for a moment. The Bandito stares at it, daring the tortilla to burn. Boom—he flips the tortilla onto a paper plate and carefully spoons the chicken into it. He folds the taco over like he's putting one of his own children to bed.

"One taco. Cheecken," he says with a smile. He takes another drag off his spliff and gives you the plate. You're quick to hand over your dollar and realize you haven't actually seen a peso since you got to Mexico.

"This looks great," Lani says to the Bandito. She turns to you, her voice suddenly a whisper. "You have to drink hard alcohol after eating this. Booze kills bacteria. It's a scientific *fact*." She looks up at the Taco Bandito and grins. "You got anything to drink?"

The Bandito uncovers a greasy bottle of tequila from his stash. "Homemade," he says. He pours two shots and gives one to each of you. The homemade liquor looks a little sketchy. You've never seen tequila look so murky. The only thing you can think of is that taco. You pick it up, feeling the warmth.

With your first delicious bite, the chilies don't kick in.

You're in the middle of your second mouthful when the evil spices bore through your taste buds and hit your brain. Hot. Very hot. You can feel it in your eyes, your lips, even your nasal cavities. It's like a nuclear reaction. Your vision blurs, your nose begins to run, and you wonder if you might faint.

"Waaaeeerrr . . ." is all you can say, imagining actual flames leaping from your mouth. Lani looks terrified. You frantically glance around the area—the only water source you see is a dripping faucet that pokes out of the side of some building—the very same faucet a three-legged feral dog was bathing under earlier.

"No! Not the water!" Lani shouts, having followed your gaze. She picks up the greasy bottle of tequila and waves it in front of your face. "*Think* about this. It's called Montezuma's Revenge. You want to spend the rest of this trip on some dirty toilet?"

Meanwhile, your teeth are trying to escape from your mouth because it's so hot in there. Your face twists in pain, your tongue triples in size. Tequila is the last thing you want. Water . . . cool, cool, water . . . God help me, you think.

You had little to do with destroying Montezuma's empire, so he can't exact his revenge on you. Take a sip of that Tijuana water and turn to page 45.

If you decide to give the home-brewed tequila a chance, pick up that bottle and chug the pain away by turning to page 163.

This guy could be the love of your life, it's just like that **Titanic** *movie: Sure your love may be doomed, but it could be hot and steamy enough to melt that iceberg. You'll never know unless you get on the boat.*

During the harrowing taxi ride through the wilds of Tijuana, you realize you have nothing to worry about. The Eagle Scout is overly nice, lighting Lani's menthol for her, even giving directions to the taxi driver in perfect Spanish. Lani keeps sending you looks that say, "He's yours, baby."

"Well, here we are," the Eagle Scout says, as he pays the driver. You and Lani look up at a giant, glistening palace of a yacht.

"Survey says . . ." you whisper as your new skipper steps onto the dock, "ding-ding-ding-ding-ding!!"

"Ahoy!" shouts the Eagle Scout, yelling to a group on board the boat. Moments later, you and Lani are living the life you have only seen on *Miami Vice* or infomercials advertising get-rich-quick schemes. There is a crowd of about two-dozen partygoers and a crew wearing stunningly handsome white dress uniforms. A horn blares as you cruise out of the harbor.

"This is fantastic," Lani says, sipping a Cadillac margarita, complete with a little umbrella. "I thought this guy was all bullshit, but this is for real."

"I think I'm in love," you say, looking around the party for your future husband. "Maybe he's at the front of the ship, doing that 'king of the world' thing and I should go make out with him."

"Yeah, where did he go?"

"We're definitely the coolest people at the party," you observe. All the other guests look older than you: men who golf and the women who love them. They're not even drinking that much.

"So . . ." Lani says, cornering the next-youngest person, a teenage kid who's turning green, "How do you know these people?"

"Know these people?" he says, eyeing her margarita. You hand him a Corona, which he sips furtively. "Man, we're here for the free television." With that cryptic remark, the sullen teen stalks off.

"What do you think he meant by that?" you ask.

"Dude, if we get a free television out of this, I am so psyched," Lani says. "Hey, how come they're all wearing the same shirt?" She points toward the cabin, where you see your Eagle Scout emerge with a couple of middle-aged types. They all wear sea foam green polos and . . . name tags. The boat slows to a quiet chug, right along the coast, which you notice is littered with partially completed condo developments.

"Can I have your attention please?" Your future husband says with a dazzling smile. Everybody turns to look at him. You and Lani grab beers, hoping this is a toast to your pending marriage. "I'd like to thank you all for being our guests out here today. As you all know, this party is about you."

"Ahh, how sweet," you say, picturing him in a tuxedo standing next to a wedding cake.

"But this party is also about the Pueblo Vista Vacation Community." The Eagle Scout points over his shoulder at a terra cotta colored development sitting on the ocean's edge. "We'd like you to become a part of *our* community."

"Oh God," Lani gasps, "he's selling timeshares."

"For the next five hours, I want you to remember, we're not just selling timeshares," Eagle Scout explains, "We're selling a way of life. A place of sanctuary for your family. A place of spirit. A place that is yours and yours alone, for four weeks out of the year."

"Wait," you whisper to Lani, wedding cake visions crumbling, "this whole thing is about *timeshares*? I can't even buy a VCR, much less a *timeshare!*" You toss your beer over the back of the boat and head for the hard liquor. Did he say five hours? "We were gonna honeymoon in Fiji," you whine, pouring stiff margaritas.

"Wrong," Lani giggles, "You were going to honeymoon at Pueblo Vista Communities."

"Grab the bottle," you whisper at Lani, who snags the biggest and most expensive bottle of tequila from behind the bar.

"There are hundreds of reasons you should invest in Pueblo Vista Communities," the Eagle Scout says, in his used-car-salesman-on-mescaline manner. "But I'm just going to give you the top fifty. Now if you'd turn to section A, page fifteen of your manuals . . ."

Somebody hands you a manual the size of a phone book. Lani tosses hers overboard in one swift throw. *Splash.* The crowd begins to settle into their seats. You are stuck. Trapped. For the next five hours. You will be beaten, you will be brainwashed, and you will try your best to resist the demonic pull of Pueblo Vista.

"How far is the swim?" you ask, eyeballing the coast.

"Too far. The sharks would get us first, but that might not be so bad."

The End

You have decided you are not to be trusted with dynamite—this is a vacation, not guerilla warfare.

You both turn away from the man with the M-80s. He suddenly becomes a very motivated seller. You can hear his desperate pleas, his frantic slashing of prices, and you don't look back—you are not even remotely interested.

"What now, mamacita?" Lani asks. "Donkey show? Illegal pharmaceuticals?"

"To tell you the truth—I am barely standing from last night. All I have in my tummy is Pabst Blue Ribbon and a couple pieces of Nicorette gum."

"Food it is!" Lani begins to guide you through the marketplace with a sense of purpose. "There is the *best* taco stand near here—and nothing is more certain to kill a nasty hangover than authentic Mexican cuisine."

"I can only assume you're using the term 'cuisine' lightly."

"Ahhh—right over here! Yes!" Lani says, dragging you through the marketplace. As you snake through a few merchants, you catch a glimpse of what she is dragging you toward: It looks like a shack with a counter, the entire structure built with straw and palm leaves. There is a fat man inside the shack with a camping barbeque grill and three rickety stools laying on their sides at the front. There are no tables, menus, or any of the other formalities spoiled gringos, or the health department, would be accustomed to.

"Are you sure this is, um, sanitary?"

"Hell, yeah," Lani replies. "On the Food Network they call

it an 'open kitchen.' This way you get to see the food being prepared. In Tijuana that's a blessing, my friend."

Skeptical as hell, you start calculating the hours until you are back in the states and can hit a Taco Bell. If you spend four more hours here, plus thirty minutes to get back to the car, fifteen minutes at the border crossing . . . How long can a person curb her hunger with menthols and Coronas?

You're about to take a seat at the shack when suddenly, a Mexican teenager materializes and thrusts a scrap of bright green paper at you. It reads:

> FREE ENCHILADA AND 2 CORONAS
> FOR EVERY MARGARITA PURCHASED!
> COME TO CAFÉ PACIFIC, VOTED BEST FOOD
> SOUTH OF THE BORDER!

Oh my God, it's a sign, a message from heaven. "Lani, look at this! It was voted best food, I mean, you know, it doesn't say it has an open kitchen, but it has critical acclaim!"

"Oh, Christ. That place is a rat hole. I vomited on the floor there when I was fourteen. Is that the kind of place you want to patronize?"

"Well . . ." You look at the fat man in the shack manning his portable barbeque, smoking a spliff. Yikes. However, Lani is probably not the first to puke at Café Pacific. You're definitely hungry, and have to admit you won't be able to subsist on cigarettes. Where did those kids selling Chicklets go?

If you trust Lani's judgment and want to see your food being prepared by the stoned grill master, turn to page 22.

If you would rather go to the critically acclaimed yet somewhat suspect Café Pacific, turn to page 124.

If you are going to go down—you will go down in a blaze of glory. It may not be pretty, it may not be safe, but you are going to take the final kamikaze shot.

"Chug, chug, chug!" your fans yell in a frenzy. Your vision's now blurry and distorted, the single shot glass morphing into two. Somehow, you manage to pick up the glass—and hold it up. The mob grows respectfully silent. You tilt your head back, pouring the liquid down your throat, and by some animal survival reflex, you manage to swallow. The crowd applauds, insane with praise. Through your haze, you try to be gracious as people slap you on the back, high-five you, and actually offer to buy you more drinks. You can't do anything but sit and smoke the most therapeutic cigarette you've had in your life.

The Ghostbuster approaches your table again. You shrink away, fearing he's come to inflict more torture by shot glass. Instead, he ties a rope around your wrist, shouting congratulations in Spanish. You gaze at the long rope that winds between bodies near the dance floor. The crowd slowly parts, revealing that the other end of the rope is wrapped around the neck of a small donkey.

"Lani," you whisper, "I drank too much. I am seeing things, more specifically, I'm seeing a pet donkey." You look at her for reassurance that your drunken hallucination is merely temporary. Instead, Lani's jaw is in her lap. She stares at the animal in disbelief.

"Good Christ, you won a baby donkey," she says. "That is

the coolest shit I have ever seen. I never knew I wanted a donkey until this very minute." Her face softens and she starts to look at the animal with great affection. "She's soooo cute—isn't she?" You cannot really judge the "cuteness" of the donkey yet, as you are still stuck on the fact it's tied to your arm. "I think we should name her Daisy." The donkey walks up to your booth and licks the surface of the table, her tongue sweeping a full pack of cigarettes into her mouth. "See?" Lani shrieks, "She likes Parliaments too!"

"Lani," you say, pointing out the obvious, "it doesn't take a naturalist to figure out this donkey is no woman. Unless it's one of those five-legged donkeys."

Lani giggles, checks out his package, but insists that you can still call him Daisy. With Daisy on your arm, you decide you'd better get out of there. And even though you have to go through ass-grab-alley to get out the door, the lecherous men do not bother you. This donkey could come in handy.

You and Lani spend the rest of your afternoon walking around Tijuana with Daisy. You never knew having a pet donkey could be so much fun! And easy! He eats hay, old newspapers, just about anything within his reach. And if you want to reward him, you feed him his very favorite snack: a Parliament cigarette. He's very calm, he barely blinks at the children that run up to him and poke him in the snout, and you can strap everything you buy at the marketplace on his back, and he doesn't mind!

The sun starts to set, and you are exhausted, sunburned, and hungry. It's time to head back to the United States. A man in a leather rancher jacket walks up to you and points at Daisy.

"You a-selling the burro? I buy for you." You look at the rancher, who pulls several twenty-dollar bills from his dusty jeans. You are about to tell the man to forget it, but Lani tells him to wait.

She looks at Daisy and sighs. "There's no way we can walk him across the border. I have never, *ever* heard of anyone bringing a donkey across."

"Why not?" you ask. "It's not like he has mad cow disease! We can't just abandon him!"

Lani looks at the sweet old rancher. "He will give him a good home, with lots of oats and grass, and other donkey friends. We can give this guy all our Parliaments to feed him when he's good."

You look into the eyes of the noble beast, your new friend. You can't imagine leaving him with a strange man, but can you really live with Daisy in America? The border patrol will surely confiscate him and he'll rot away in donkey prison. The future of this donkey's life rests in your hands.

If you sell the donkey and let it roam greener pastures, turn to page 148.

Daisy is coming home with you! Try to sneak a 300-pound beast past the border and turn to page 140.

"We could never say no to a birthday," you say, as Lani digs the heel of her shoe into your pinky toe. You smile through the tears. Don Chicklet grins.

Before you know it, you're riding in a plush Chicklet-pink Cadillac with leather seats and climate control—the works. Where cup holders should be, there are little dishes of Chicklets.

"This guy is off his mother-grabbin' rocker," Lani whispers.

Don Chicklet is like Moses with his staff, parting the red sea of people as the Caddy winds its way through the crowded Tijuana streets and up into the scrubby hills above the city. After passing through a gate, you're headed toward a massive estate. Everything's pale pink, a perfect match for the car.

"*Ay, Dios mío,*" you say as the mansion comes into view. "Welcome to the house that chewing gum built." The driveway is crowded with kids and families and young adults. Lavish decorations and party streamers are everywhere. Surely Chicklet distribution is a legitimate business.

When Don Chicklet gets out of his car, he's greeted like royalty. A sizzlin' hot young stud trots up to you and Lani. "Don Chicklet has told me if you ladies need anything, I am to help you. My name is Julio." He flashes a smile. This guy would beat Antonio Banderas in a beauty contest. You notice Lani has cheered up considerably.

"Julio, could you show a couple of gringos like us where we could get a margarita?" Lani purrs.

"Follow me," Julio says. Then he winks at you. At you! Before you can introduce yourself, Lani grabs your hand and races after him. You follow Julio through the crowded dance floor, and then find yourselves at the bar. This birthday party has got to be one of the most incredible, expensive, huge parties you've ever seen. They have everything here, from generic beer to the most expensive Petron tequila, and it's all flowing freely. "Petron margaritas?" Julio suggests.

"Sounds fantastic," Lani gushes.

"Do you like salt?" Julio asks you. Was there a suggestive tone there? What exactly does he mean by "salt" anyway?

"I *love* salt," you reply. Why the hell not? As Julio tends to your drinks, Lani spins around to face you, all business.

"Okay. He likes both of us, right?"

You thought he was vibing on you, but . . . "Yeah. You're right. I mean, who can resist hot women like us?"

"I think we should decide who gets Julio."

"Shouldn't *Julio* decide?" you offer, trying to be diplomatic.

"Fuck that," Lani says. "We are strong women who make our own decisions. But, you know . . . I've always had a thing for Latin guys."

"Since *when*!?"

"Uh . . . recently," Lani tries.

Julio has gotten your drinks. He flashes his cute little smile to both of you, which makes you swoon. He's the hottest guy at the whole party, there's a slight language barrier, he's from an exotic culture, and he lives in another country. Perfect. Even if things get weird, you'll never have to see him again.

"I don't know, Lani . . ."

"We can't risk our friendship over this. But we have to decide."

He's cute, but maybe he's not that cute. Right? Right? Lani would be so thankful she would buy you drinks for a month if it works out. Be a good friend and let Lani have the guy by turning to page 54.

She'd pout for five minutes, but Lani tends to forget about this stuff after the third drink. Break it to Lani that he's yours and turn to page 100.

Your new theme song is "Smuggler's Blues" by that guy who was much better when he was with the Eagles. You agree to take the ceramic monkey and make a run for the border.

"Okay," Scarface explains for the fifth time, "the man will find you on the other side. He knows you have the monkey. As soon as you make the exchange, your little friend will be given her passport and can go."

"Promise on the life of your mother," you demand, "the woman who endured the pain of childbirth and fed you at her breast in hope that you would grow up and live a better life than the one you've chosen."

"*Si.* On the life of *mi madre,*" Scarface says, eyes misty.

"You gonna tell me what's in the monkey?" you ask him.

"Just get it across the border," Scarface replies. He's got a point. What business is it of yours?

"Hey girlfriend, be careful," Lani says weakly.

"Next time we'll try Canada," you say, trying to sound upbeat.

Scarface hands you the ceramic monkey as his thugs drag Lani into a van that looks like the one that crazy put-the-lotion-in-the-basket guy had in *The Silence of the Lambs.* Lani's fate totally depends on you now. You hope she won't end up as the ass of some suit made of human flesh.

The border crossing looms ahead of you. The crowd bottlenecks into turnstiles manned by customs officials and border guards. This should be easy. "I'm just a normal girl coming into the United States with a ceramic surfing monkey," you reassure yourself, as you fall in line behind a cute family. Looking ahead, they don't really seem to be checking anybody at all. They just look at your passport or visa and let you pass through. It's kind of like getting into a nightclub. Yeah, you're going to Club America!

You're beginning to sweat. You try not to throw up like you did that one time you had to give a speech in fifth grade. The family in front of you goes through, showing their bags to the customs people. Suddenly, it's your turn. *Try to breathe.*

"Are you a citizen of the United States?" asks the border guard.

"Yes. I was born there," you reply, sliding your passport to her.

"Okay . . ." she begins to say, when a red light blazes on from somewhere. In an instant, the room is full of border guards and customs officials.

"What's going on?" you whimper.

"Random check. We do it every so often. Would you step aside please?"

Before you know it, a manly border guard has pulled you aside to a long metal table. He puts the ceramic monkey on the table and runs one of those metal-detector wands over you. It doesn't really beep at all, and you're sure you are free to go. Damn, this is going to be one insane story. Then he picks up the monkey and feels the weight. He hands it to his buddy. "But that's my . . ." you start to say, then decide it's better not to claim ownership. One of the guards puts the monkey on a conveyer belt, sending it through an x-ray machine. When the monkey is in the belly of the machine, the guards start shouting, looking at the image. Like most people when they know they are about to be busted, you just start thinking of good excuses.

Things get a little fuzzy in your head as you swoon in and out of your physical body. But something brings you back to reality: the cold steel of the handcuffs.

The kind men of the United States Customs haven't really been too forthcoming. The ceramic monkey didn't carry drugs in it—it had a small roll of microfilm hidden inside, protected by a titanium cylinder. Apparently, the guy you were supposed to meet was the henchman for some Mexican mafia warlord, and the microfilm was a blueprint for the entire cartel. When you explain the situation, it's only a matter of minutes before the Mexican SWAT team rescues Lani and you're hailed as a hero. Your lame performance at the border has brought down one of Mexico's most notorious drug cartels.

"Dude," Lani whispers to you as the DEA pins medals on you both, "does this mean the price of marijuana's going up again?"

The End

You simply can't resist the thought of going home with a big sack of weed. Get ready to do a drug deal in Mexico!

"Lani," you say as you put down the Diet-Coke handbag, "I am going to be strong. I am not going to give in to the sparkly power of that purse." She nods in agreement. You turn on your heels and walk away from the best bargain in North America. As you start to head back to the pharmacy, you feel your heart pumping in anticipation. Statistically, this will be your first drug deal in a foreign country, first drug deal with a stranger, and first drug deal in a back alley. You turn the corner toward the back of the pharmacy.

"Lani," you say, "we can pull this off, right?"

"Absolutely," she says, "what could possibly go wrong? Back-alley drug deals are practically legal in Mexico."

"Really?"

"Sure! We just have to meet in an alley as a formality."

"Like a cultural thing."

"Yeah, a cultural thing," she says. "Wait, I think this is the back door to the pharmacy."

You are standing in a narrow alley that runs the length of the block near a puddle of what you hope is water. There is a large dumpster and trash piles everywhere. This is one of those alleys where the rats look like cats; you gently remind yourself not to pet anything. Lani shoves a menthol in your mouth and tells you to act "casual." At least the cigarette smoke masks the incredible odor of the trash and piss and God knows what else.

The door opens and the pharmacist steps out into the alley. He lights a cigarette and says, "Let's take a walk."

You head toward the opposite end of the alley. He walks beside you, smoking. He's not looking at you. "Don't speak, just keep walking."

Wow, this is heavy, you think. You remind yourself this is a cultural thing and this is the norm of drug deals in Mexico. It's not like America, where all you have to do is go to some dude's apartment, give him forty bucks, and try out your new goods on his three-foot glass bong. Sadly, this is a much more impersonal experience.

"In a few moments, I am going to drop something," he continues, "You will pick it up without looking at it and put it away. Then you will shake my hand and give me eighty American dollars. Got it?"

"Thanks so much for helping us out," you say, feeling something drop near your toes. You snatch the baggie of weed off the alley floor and shove it into your purse. You fish around for the cash, wad it up, and shake his hand, slipping him the money. God, you are smooth! He turns and walks back to the pharmacy, and you continue toward the end of the alley with Lani. You feel a wave of exhilaration and triumph. You cannot believe you just pulled that off! Lani grabs your arm and you practically skip out of the alley.

Ten minutes later you're celebrating over margaritas, toasting your new status as an international drug maven!

"I want to see it," Lani says. "Just for a second."

"Okay, but just for a second. I don't want to be caught with this shit," you say as you hand it to her under the table. She unrolls the baggie on her lap.

"What's this?" she asks. In the middle of the weed is another smaller pouch. It's filled with white powder.

"Oh shit," you say, "how the hell should I know? Put it away!" Lani hands it back to you.

"I don't do white powders," Lani explains, "and I'm sure that's not baking soda."

"Let's get the hell out of here. This is a major buzzkill." Lani waves for the check and a young male waiter approaches the table.

"Thank you, ladies," he says, handing you the bill. He sees the baggie as you try to hide it away. "And . . . I know someone who can help you get rid of that stuff, if you know what I mean." You try to look shocked.

"I don't know what you are talking about."

"Of course not," he smiles, "just a thought."

He leaves and you gather your things. As you take your last swallow of margarita, you begin to consider his offer. You have no idea what is in that bag, and this may be your only chance to unload it. And you do *not* want to be caught bringing it into the States.

If you decide one drug deal is not enough for one day, talk to the waiter and arrange another transaction! Turn to page 70.

If you would rather take your chances in the good old US of A, make a run for the border and turn to page 106.

Tangle in Tijuana

Left without passports or cash, you and Lani are screwed. When you call home collect, your friends just laugh, thinking it's a joke. Some joke. You're stranded in Tijuana.

"I have to say I have a real sympathy for these people that I don't think I had before now," Lani says.

You and Lani are packed into the back of Mexico's oldest pickup truck, sitting with a dozen of your newest friends. The closest thing to a seatbelt here is a rope that you let the youngest kid hold on to. Nobody speaks English, but there's not much to say. You're making a run for the border, and this ain't no Taco Bell.

As the sun dips below the horizon, the truck picks up speed. You're in the middle of the desert now. There are no roads you can see, just tire tracks and debris from previous crossings. Signs in Spanish warn you to turn back, but you're going for it.

"There's the border," you say to Lani. In the distance, when the hills break, you can spot fluorescent lights along the top of a fence. When the truck finally stops, you're officially carsick, but there's no time to rest. Everybody leaps out and moves through the darkness, the driver of the pickup leaves you to fend for yourself.

"*Vámonos,*" a nice older woman says, gesturing for the two of you to follow her. Nobody dares say a word after that. The group is as quiet as mice, the only sound is Lani stumbling over rocks in her sandals.

After a half hour of hiking, you hear the sound of rushing water. Lani hands you a cigarette, which you light, take a drag off of, and hand to a fourteen-year-old boy. In the darkness, you can sense you're not the only people here at this spot. It's a favorite border crossing. Your eyes adjust to the moonlight. In the distance is a chain-link fence with hurricane razor wire on the top. Beyond the razor wire is a river about fifty yards wide, and past that is one more fence and then—the American dream.

Lani and you crouch down, waiting for the right moment. "Fuck this designer sandal bullshit," Lani says. She takes off her sandals and tosses them over the fence and into the river. "This is real life. *Real life.*"

Somewhere, you hear a bird call—it's the signal. You and everybody else rush at the fence. The fourteen-year-old cigarette smoker leads the charge, throwing a horse blanket over the razor wire. You climb sure and fast, remembering how you used to do this to sneak onto school grounds and into closed parks. You make it over the razor wire without injury. The kid makes sure you and Lani are over okay before grabbing the horse blanket.

The water, thank God, isn't running very fast. The boy looks a little scared. The kid's probably never swam in his life. You reach out your hand to him. "I've got you," you assure him, hoping he understands. You and Lani wade into the river, the kid between you. The other border crossers hold hands, making a human chain. They whisper nervously, everybody hurrying along, scared out of their minds. You gulp air, trying to stay afloat as you drift toward the other side of the river.

Finally, your toes touch land. The kid's still with you, freaked out but happy to be alive. You point toward the last chain-link fence. Everybody is so tired, you wonder how anybody ever gets across at all. Then comes a shout from down river.

"Policía!!" You can hear the sound of trucks. You and Lani freeze.

"We can do this," you tell her. "We are danger girls."

Lani grins and turns to the kid. "Let's roll," she says.

"Danger girls," he says in broken English. The three of you rush for the fence, the kid doing his thing with the blanket. You're the last one over the fence. When the spotlight hits the chain link, the only thing the border guards catch is a wet horse blanket.

Upon your successful return to the United States of America, you and Lani can't help but look at things differently—the two of you love your country and want to share it with the world. After a late night full of tequila and promises, you make a decision: You will be the most badass immigration lawyers in the American southwest. Partying is still on the agenda, but it seems to all be worth more because you have a goal. In five years you and Lani will be working together in an office in San Diego, laughing about how it took a trip to Mexico to make you understand how special the American Dream is.

The End

All those stories about the water in Mexico must be an exaggeration, I mean, it is the 21st century and all the locals seem healthy, so you decide to go for it.

You grab a dirty cup from the taco guy's stand and race to the water faucet, your mouth on fire. The mangy dog sees you coming and tries to defend his watering hole, but you bare your own teeth.

"*Vámonos!*" you hiss at the cur. He backs away, having felt the heat of your breath and having seen the desperate look in your eyes. The faucet is easy to turn on, and the lukewarm water gushes out full blast. After a moment of silent prayer, you fill the cup and start drinking, feeling like there is steam coming out of your ears as the heat subsides.

"Ohmigod!" Lani screams, scrambling over. "Stop that!"

You shake her off, gulping down another cup of water. The sweating has begun to subside, your tongue is returning to its normal size. After a gallon of Tijuana's finest water, you can breathe normally.

"I . . . I'm okay . . ."

"No. No, you're not," Lani says, nervously.

"This is not the Ebola virus," you say, rolling your eyes.

"Yeah it is. I read that book, people bleed out of their eyes and shit out their kidneys! You might as well have licked the fur of a diseased spider monkey!"

The two of you head off into the main drag, watching the vendors hock their wares. Lani stays a few steps from you, like she expects to catch something. You practically have to yell to talk to her.

"All I did was drink the water!" you shout at her.

People all around you are beginning to snicker. A tourist family points at you like you're a leper. That's when you feel the first wave. You stop walking. Suddenly you feel weak in the knees, your equilibrium vanishes. "What's going on?" you mutter to yourself. The last time you puked was sophomore year in high school when Denny Scofield fed you Long Island Iced Teas and tried to give you his virginity. Instead, Denny ended up spending all night watching you puke into his mother's toilet. Whatever's going on in your digestive system right now is ten times worse than the Denny Scofield incident.

"Hey, is something wrong?" Lani asks, backtracking to you. "Oh man, you're white as a sheet," she says.

Another wave of nausea hits you. Somewhere, in the fabric of the space-time continuum, you can hear Montezuma himself mocking you for your hubris.

"It wasn't me who killed your people," you plead. "I wasn't even born yet!" Lani now thinks you're insane. One glance around the street and you realize you are a ship lost at sea with no friendly port to dock in. Lani leaves you for a moment, asking a guy who sells ceramic Chihuahuas where you can find a bathroom. After he stops laughing, he points down the street to the darkest corner of the industrialized world. Lani takes your clammy hand and leads you. You barely hear her as she says, "It's a public toilet . . ." which sounds to you like "blah blah blah blah *toilet* . . ." You arrive at a bathroom that makes you ache for the comfort of even the worst Porta-Potty after a day-long music festival.

"I'm gonna hurl," you say. "I don't need a toilet."

"Yeah, you do. They can put you in jail if you puke or piss in public. That's what the ceramic Chihuahua man said."

Your guts do a horrific back flip as you look at your options: a disgusting shack with a rusty metal door and an odor from another world, or the public street. There isn't even a trashcan in the vicinity. People are beginning to stare as you double over, moaning. Somewhere, you can hear a group of guys laughing. You look up to see the same group of obnoxious frat guys who heckled you on the freeway near the border. One of them screams something about a video camera—"Hurry up, this chick's gonna spew!"

"Fuck off, Fratty," Lani says, "go find a donkey show to tape, perv."

As the chunks rise up in your throat, you picture yourself puking in public, puking on camera, and probably puking on the Internet. Then again, there is a private but scary Tijuana toilet within minimum safe distance. Choose fast; Montezuma's Revenge is an eminent uprising . . .

Let the world see what you ate today! Bend over, take a deep breath, and turn to page 67.

If you think your stomach contents are for your eyes only, take refuge from open ridicule in a public toilet by turning to page 149.

You are not going to be the pathetic loser nursing tequila by yourself. You are going to your first bachelor party!

"Glen, I will join you and your friends," you say, "under one condition. I am not jumping out of a huge cake."

"What the hell are you talking about?" he asks you, incredulous. You make a note: Do not attempt humor around Glen. As you leave the club, you tell Lani to call you on your cell when she "comes up for air." She looks confused as you turn on your heel and leave.

Outside the club, the men in the bachelor party all light up cigars and practically shove each other off the sidewalk in an attempt to be close to you. They want to know everything about you, and seem to listen with as much genuine interest as drunkards can muster. You feel like the modern Scarlet O'Hara, holding court with all these gentlemen.

The group enters another nightclub, led by the man you assume is the groom-to-be. He is easy to spot, since he is a) the drunkest of the group and b) being forced to wear a pink tutu over his shorts. The owner of the club seats you at several tables, and when you put down your purse, you notice the floor is covered in straw. What kind of place is this? Two shots later, and more on the way, you are killing the men with your arsenal of jokes about quadriplegics. As three men all whip out their lighters to spark your cigarette, stage lights come up in the front of the club. You didn't even notice there was a stage until now.

A man wearing a ridiculous matador coat jumps up and

starts babbling in Spanish into a microphone. You don't grasp exactly what he is saying, but you have the sinking sensation that you are about to watch some sort of sleazy burlesque show. Thank God you are drunk. You lean over to a guy next to you and ask, "What is this?"

"You mean no one told you?" He seems slightly horrified and amused at the same time.

"Is this some ping-pong ball show?" you ask, suspiciously. "You know, me-love-you-long-time kind of shit?" He opens his mouth like he is going to speak, but then turns away to give his attention to the stage.

A woman in nothing more than a bra and a very short skirt struts around the stage to some hyperactive Mexican song. All the men in the club hoot, which you think is weird because the woman is well into her 40s and overweight. Suddenly the matador sweeps a red cape around, and onto the stage he lures, not a toro, but a donkey. The poor animal looks heavily sedated and incoherently clomps on the rickety stage. Before you can whisper "the horror, the horror," the woman rubs her tits on either side of the donkey's snout while the man straps some device around the body of the beast. The crowd is going nuts, chanting "Burro, burro!"

This is your cue to leave.

"Excuse me," you shout over the din, "I am *so* out of here!"

The guys don't even notice you leaving, but perhaps that is because they are busy ogling a woman who has climbed onstage to position herself underneath the drugged donkey. Yikes. You grab your purse, two cigars, some guy's aviator shades, and a full jumbo-size margarita to go.

Outside, you feel like you have just escaped the shit storm

to end all shit storms. Witnessing an act of bestiality would take years of therapy to undo. You slip on your newly stolen shades, cram the cigars into your purse, and slug your drink gratefully. As you stumble back toward Mamacita's, you can't help but feel you've learned an invaluable lesson. You would rather watch Lani get it on with your boy-toy than watch depraved beastiality any day.

The End

Will you spend the rest of the year sneezing and wheezing, just to take a little blue pill of horniness? Hell yes!

"Here you go, pervert," you say to Lani, handing her a wad of cash. In return, the pharmacist passes her a bottle of little blue magic. Lani holds the bottle in careful wonderment—like it contains the secrets of cold fusion. "Don't get all hot and bothered yet," you tell her, "I hear it doesn't even work if you're under fifty."

"There's only one way to find out," Lani says. "Let's get a drink."

You find a table near a fountain in a marketplace courtyard. A waitress in a frilly Mexican outfit serves you two rainbow-colored frozen margaritas, blended to perfection. "A toast," you say, lifting up your cup, "may your chemically enhanced libido bring you to new orgasmic heights."

Clinking your glass, Lani squeals, "I'll drink to that."

"So will I," a voice chimes in. You look up to see a young man with a stubbly chin and messy mop of hair. He has green eyes, a big crooked nose, and a goofy smile. The sum total of the parts makes him good looking in an unconventional way. Lani nearly knocks you over to greet him.

"Hello, gorgeous," she says, never one for subtlety. "Why don't you join us?" The man motions for his friend to come over. While he is turned away, Lani mouths to you *"He's hot."*

Mr. Green Eyes sits next to you and introduces himself as Jesse. His friend is a little pudgy around the edges and for some reason thinks it's okay to wear sweatpants in public. He smokes one of an unending chain of cigarettes, hurriedly introducing himself as Bill. To your amusement, Jesse ignores Lani and her suddenly prominent cleavage, and flirts with you instead.

While Bill and Lani leave to go get margarita refills, you discover you and Jesse have almost nothing in common. For instance, he loves reptiles, skateboarding, and trip-hop music. You like puppies, sailing, and Madonna. But you figure since the two of you are so different, you could learn a lot from him. Like what a leopard gecko is.

Lani and Bill return and place two frozen margaritas in front of you. Grinning a Cheshire Cat smile, Lani says, "Button, button, who's got the button?"

"What is this?" you ask, looking at the two beverages. One frosty drink is green, and one is pink.

"Don't you remember?" Bill says, "Those early eighties anti-drug books? The bad crowd kids would always play that game at parties?"

"Everyone got a soda—but one of the sodas was dosed," Lani continues.

"Oh yeah," you say, "and someone got drugged, and the game was called Button!"

"Right!" Lani yells, "So my question to you is, who's got the button?" You glance down at the margaritas and understand. One of the drinks is dosed with a little blue pill.

"You lost a button?" Jesse asks. He's cute, but not so bright. You pat his knee and give him a reassuring smile. Maybe its best you take the bullet and save him an aching boner for the rest of the day. Besides, you hear Viagra is great for women too.

Bill and Lani stifle giggles as you examine your situation. There's the old standby, the green margarita, and then there's the strawberry margarita. Would Lani dose a regular one thinking you would choose it or would she drug the pink one thinking one step ahead of you? Should you even bother to ascribe any rhyme or reason to a girl that would drug you with Viagra in the first place?

"Pick one before it melts," Lani says with a wicked grin.

Green means go! Slug down the green machine and turn to page 122.

You have always liked pink—for your clothes, your fancy soaps, your toenail polish, so why not your margarita? Think pink and turn to page 132.

"He's yours. You take him," you whisper. God, you're such a good friend you deserve a plaque or something.

Any idea that Julio was only interested in you immediately vanishes the second Lani whispers in his ear. He smiles at her, enraptured, totally ignoring you. " . . . I volunteer three times a week at the local children's hospital . . ." Julio mentions to Lani. What an asshole.

Lani and Julio don't notice as you take your leave of them. All around you, people are having fun, enjoying themselves. Little kids are chowing down on food and cake, dancing around you and generally spoiling your bad mood. You hand one of them your margarita and tell him its candy, taking a seat with your new best friend—a tequila bottle. "I declare this table property of *me!*" you explain to the waiter who serves you a piece of cake. The cake (decorated with Chicklets) looks great, but the tequila is all the nourishment you need. Everybody swirls around you, laughing and smiling. It's disgusting. When you notice a Funsaver camera at the center of the table, you briefly consider taking a photo of your ass.

How you got from that table to the fringes of Don Chicklet's ranch is beyond you, but that's the magic of binge drinking. You never know where you're gonna end up. The sun hangs low on the horizon. One of the last things you remember is taking a picture of the sunset with your Funsaver camera.

"Mmmmmaaaaaaaaaaa!" A disturbing sound wakes you up. You've passed out under a tree on Don Chicklet's ranch. All

around you, ranch animals are beginning to panic. Horses pound the ground with their hooves, chickens begin to squawk, the cows actually make an effort to move. Something is wrong. You quietly make your way along the fences, toward a pen perched on the fringes of the canyon. That's where that awful sound came from.

"*MmmmMMMAAAhhhh!*" screams a goat, racing past you. You almost pee yourself. That goat was scared out of its mind! In the darkness, you can make out the outline of dozens of goats, all of them running from something. But one baby goat is too slow. You watch in horror as something leaps at it from the darkness.

Wham! Baby goat goes *down*! It emits a horrified shriek as you race to help it, and then you see what attacked it. You stop dead in your tracks. This is no coyote.

"*El Chupacabras,*" you whisper.

Crouched over the goat is a goblinlike creature the size of a large dog. It has scaly skin and talons that glint in the moonlight. Like any good kid who went to summer camp and believed in urban legends, you have heard stories about El Chupacabras. He's the Bigfoot of Latin countries and the Loch Ness monster of the Southwest, a creature that sucks the blood out of goats like a vampire. You have also heard about this monster from reliable sources like *The X-Files* and your conspiracy-obsessed ex-boyfriend.

You can only think of one thing. The Funsaver camera.

"Leave the kid alone!" you shout at El Chupacabras. He puts his head up and hisses at you like a snake. *Flash*. You take a picture, blinding the beast. *Flash*. You take another one. As you keep taking pictures, he seems confused and scared, backing away from the goat and your magical flashy thing. With one last hiss, he bounds over a fence and into the canyons. You look down at the Funsaver in your hands. You have just taken photographic proof of El Chupacabras.

Back in the states a few months later, all the world is talking about your Pulitzer Prize–winning photographs of El Chupacabras. Your Funsaver photos are on T-shirts, mugs, and billboards—it's a phenomenon. None of your friends care that Lani and Julio eloped to Vegas and got divorced a week later, all they care about is how fucking cool you are for giving the world a glimpse of El Chupacabras. Aside from the lifetime supply of Funsavers and your brilliant performance in their national commercial, you've been offered jobs all over the world. Organizations want to hire you to track down the abominable snowman and UFOs. Maybe you'll give it a shot, but first you plan to travel for a while, making the big bucks on the lecture circuit. And you'll *never* go anywhere near a goat farm ever again.

The End

Fuck tha po-lice, you think. The cops will be no help to you, and your creepy new fren' seems to know something.

"Alright señor," you say in your "don't mess with me" voice, "tell us what you know about the car."

He smiles a toothy gold grin and says smugly, "I tell you, but it's going to cost you."

Gritting your teeth you say, "I am going to give you twenty American dollars, and if you don't spill, I'm yelling rape. *Comprende?*"

You hand over the twenty, and your newfound fren' motions you to follow him. Lani staggers along with you in a catatonic stupor, as you follow this shady character into the bowels of Tijuana.

While repeatedly shoving cigarettes in her mouth, you keep telling Lani bullshit like: "This is a real adventure!" and "We're going to laugh about this one day . . ." and "I'm sure this will all be over soon and we'll be celebrating over margaritas."

You are telling Lani to go to her "happy place" for the fifth time when you notice that you are approaching a large crowd of people. It looks like a high-school football game with families on rickety bleachers and crowds standing shoulder to shoulder around an arena.

"What is it?" Lani asks. And then you hear it. The unmistakable sound of engines running, revving and peeling around wildly. Then *crunching* metal. Your jaw drops. You know what this is. You've read about it in books but didn't know it actually existed in the modern world until now. "What is it?" Lani pleads again.

"A demolition derby," you say solemnly.

"*Nooooo!!!!*" Lani yells, as she breaks through the crowd. You follow her past the hordes of men holding beers in their hands and children on their shoulders. You finally catch up with her against a chain-link fence at the edge of the arena.

In the center of the pit, there are two cars flipped over and demolished. An orange muscle car with no doors is chasing an old white sedan in circles, trying to slam it into submission. Two other cars have tangled bumpers and can't be separated, bound by twisted metal. And then to the left—you see it: It's Lani's car alright, but the front of it has been painted with a toothy, sharklike grin.

"At least it looks like you're winning," you say meekly.

"*Run, run away!*" Lani screams at her car, hoping it will respond to the sound of her voice. However, Lani's car is no Herbie the Love Bug. It listens to whoever is at the wheel, and right now it appears to be a fourteen-year-old Mexican boy with a death wish.

Wham! The white sedan rams one of the tangled cars, sending it into a 360 spin. The crowd goes wild. Before you can pretend this is not exciting (for Lani's sake), the dizzy car hangs its white flag, surrendering. There are only three cars left. Lani's seems to be stuck in the mud. The other two cars smell its weakness.

"Oh no, Lani," you say, but she is no longer beside you. She has made her way over the fence and is running into the pit! You notice she is still carrying her evergreen tree air freshener.

"*Run, Lani!*" you scream. Lani dashes through the demolished vehicles to her car. You can't hear what she's saying over the deafening sound of engines, but by the time she's torn the Mexican kid out of her car, the boy is crying.

The two other cars circle like wolves. They aren't going to let Lani out of this one with a full transmission. Lani, ecstatic to be reunited with her car, is grinning and kissing her steering wheel. She is oblivious to the two angry drivers on either side of her, thirsty to take her down.

Vrooom. Vrooooom. The cars roar to each other in agreement. You look down, unable to watch. Opening your eyes, you see salvation: the bag full of M-80s at your feet. You tear the package open and grab a handful of dynamite sticks. You fumble for your lighter, then think better of it and grab a cigarillo out of some guy's mouth.

"Bitch is *loco*!!!" he screams, realizing what you're doing.

That's right, you think as you light the M-80s and let the wick burn down a little. *This bitch is fucking loco.*

The two cars accelerate toward Lani. You calculate their speed like a quarterback. You loft the first stick of dynamite to your left, then turn and launch the other one to your right. They fly through the air, turning over as the wick burns lower and lower. "Step on it, Lani!" you shout. Lani's eyes go wide as she realizes what you've just done. She hits the gas.

Boom! Booooom!

Twin explosions rock the arena. Your hair blows back and you can feel the heat. Smoke is everywhere. Little children are crying and somewhere a woman wails, "*Muertos!*"

I've killed Lani, you think. A gust of wind blows some of the smoke away, and a giant sharklike grin emerges from the dark clouds. Blaring her horn, Lani drives out of the smoke, unharmed. Your heart leaps. Lani plows through the chain-link fence and stops three feet from you.

"Get in!" she screams. You scramble into the car, holding an M-80 out as a weapon. The crowd hangs back, terrified. Lani hits the gas and kicks up dust behind you. She switches on the radio, which is tuned to a Mexican radio station. You take a drag of the strange man's cigarillo, smiling.

"Let's get the fuck outta Mexico," you say through blue smoke.

"Adios," Lani says.

The End

Perhaps you've had too much time in the sun, because you have decided to go along on a coke run.

"Alright," you say to Jaws. "We're in. But if any shit goes down, you drugged and kidnapped me and I have no mother-grabbing idea what's going on. Got it?"

"Got it, babe," Jaws grins, "now chill. Do a line?"

You roll your eyes and turn away, opting for your pack of Parliaments. "I will get high the way God intended," you tell him, "on cigarettes and booze."

You join Lani on the deck as the boat chugs up to a small dock. It looks like you're on the outskirts of a large town. This is seedy already. Jaws, Guy, and the Guys emerge from the cabin of the boat carrying duffel bags. "Subtle," you say under your breath.

"Where are you going?" Lani whines to Jaws.

"We ran out of tortilla chips and margarita mix," he says, shooting you a look. "Gotta make a run." Lani seems satisfied. You bite your tongue, resisting the urge to tell Lani her new boyfriend is the Pusher Man.

The men leave the boat and walk down the dock. When they are out of view, you light up and ask Lani the question of the day: "What would you do with twenty-thousand dollars?"

"I would invest in a monster truck," she says, with no hesitation. "I would call it *The Pacifist*. We would tour the world . . ."

"Damn. I was going to say high-risk mutual funds, but now that seems so lame."

You start to wonder what you would do with twenty thou. I mean, it's nice cash for a day's work lounging around in a boat, but it's really not *that* much money in the grand scheme of things. Maybe you should spend half of it on serious investments, and half of it on a pool table and a Sharper Image massage chair. You are about to break the news to Lani about the coke deal when you catch her trying to smoke the Parliament through one of her nostrils. Damn, she is drunker than you thought.

"Look what I can do!" She squeals, the cigarette hanging from her nose. She is in no shape to understand the gravity of the situation. You are keeping this info to yourself. You lie on the boat deck for what seems like hours, wondering if you'll be incarcerated at any moment.

When you hear men climbing aboard, you run to the side of the boat, heart pumping wildly. Thank the lord, it's Jaws, Guy, and the Guys. Guy gives you a thumbs-up. You literally shriek and jump for joy. Once everyone is on board, the boat pulls away from the dock and heads back toward Tijuana. Guy slips his arm around your waist and kisses you.

"I got something for you," he says, and stuffs a brick of bills down your cleavage. You squeal and hug him. You are *so* Bonnie and Clyde.

Jaws shocks Lani by handing her a huge stack of bills. Without asking any questions, she puts the cash in her purse, smiles sweetly, and says, "Thanks, but I was probably going to fuck you anyway."

Nine months later, you and Lani sit front-row center at the Rosemont Horizon Stadium outside Chicago. Surrounding you is a mob of crazed Monster Truck Rally fans screaming, *"Fist! Fist!"* and pumping their fists in the air. A huge truck roars into the dirt arena.

"That's our baby," you yell over the din. Lani points proudly. The monster truck is Barbie-doll pink, and on the side it reads "The Paci-FIST." The hood displays an elaborate air-brushed cartoon of two busty women holding up their fists. It is girl power meets horsepower.

It revs its blisteringly loud engine, and proceeds to decimate row upon row of unfortunate cars. This trip to Chicago is the first of many stops you and Lani will hit on the Monster Truck circuit. The two of you raise your cheap draft beers in a toast. Now that you have conquered Mexico together, it's time to see how much trouble you can find in your own country.

The End

Say good-bye to Toothy Guy, and explore your other options . . .

You land at a small table with a "reserved" sign on it, which Lani takes and puts in her purse as "a souvenir." This has got to be the best table in the place. You're directly at the edge of the dance floor, close to the bar, and far away from ass-grab-alley. You order up some margaritas and scope out the place.

In the midst of a heated conversation about why straight men should never wear white jeans, the lights dim, and creepy horror music starts to blare throughout the club. It sounds like a bad haunted-house soundtrack, but it must mean something because all the people on the dance floor start freaking out. A spotlight frames a figure in the middle of the crowd, and the *Ghostbusters* theme starts up. You stand on your chair to see a Mexican man wearing a gray jumpsuit, à la *Ghostbusters,* and a huge tank on his back. In his hands, two tubes running from the contraption start squirting liquid into the open mouths of the dancers.

"Holy shit, dude," Lani yells, "get that little goofball over here!" She stands up and flails her arms around like it's an emergency. The Ghostbuster catches her eye and boogies toward your table. As the crowd sings along to the song, "Who you gonna call? Ghostbusters!" Lani opens her mouth like a hungry baby chick. The Ghostbuster squirts an arc of clear liquid in the air which lands perfectly in her mouth. The crowd chants, "Chug, chug!" and Lani continues to do just that for about thirty seconds straight. When she finally comes up for air, she is greeted with exuberant applause.

The Ghostbuster sets his sights on you and removes *five* shot glasses from his utility belt. He lines up the glasses in front of you and pours a shot. The crowd stares at you, waiting. You take the shot without wincing, and the crowd screams. As you secretly try not to gag, you ask Lani, "What is this shit?"

"Kamikaze," she whispers. The Ghostbuster pours another shot and you throw it back with gusto. As you lift the *third* shot glass, your stomach backflips, but you take it down anyway. That one gave you the shivers, but you try to shake it off by stealing the cigarette out of Lani's mouth and taking a drag. The smoke calms your stomach, but you know you are furiously wasted. And the crowd is counting on you. The Ghostbuster hands you the fourth shot and you suddenly understand why this shit is called "Kamikaze." You feel like you are heading for a brick wall at sixty miles per hour.

"*Chug, Chug!*" The crowd screams. You're a sucker for peer pressure. You throw it back and manage to swallow, but just barely. You feel your stomach start to rebel, and you taste bile in the back of your throat. Your jaw tightens, and you *know* you are about to hurl. You place your hands on the top of your head, and take a few deep relaxation breaths. This old trick works, and the nausea subsides. You smile weakly at the crowd and give a half-assed drunken thumbs up. Oh no. You look down and see the Ghostbuster has poured you your fifth and final shot.

You've narrowly averted disaster by not puking in front of this crowd, and one more shot might put you over the edge. You look to the sky and wonder if this is the kind of decision that God gives input on. Lani offers her own advice, calmly telling you not to take the final shot. But you can hear the crowd screaming, they want more! You're their hero! How can you disappoint your adoring public?

You are already wasted—what is one more shot at this point? Win the crowd over. Take that last shot and turn to page 30.

You are not going to be Puking Kamikaze Girl for the rest of this trip. Humbly decline the final shot and turn to page 161.

There is no way you're going into that steel trap of a bathroom. Even if you have to show the world what happens when good water goes bad.

"Hurl! Hurl! Hurl! Hurl!" the fratboys chant. This is probably not the first time these future dads and CEOs have sung this particular chant.

"Moooove!" you scream, heading for the alley. The fratboys give chase like a pack of wolves that sense you're the weak one in the herd. You stumble into the shade, the smell of rotting chicken carcasses enveloping you. Now, sadly, is the time to hurl.

Bleeeeeccchhh. You've never felt such a horrible thing in all your life. You never really thought about the phrase "puke your guts out" until that very moment. The fratboys zoom in with their camera, pushing Lani aside. Your taco and the diseased water spill out onto the alley, mixing with whatever other putrid thing was there before.

"Assholes! Can't you see she's sick?" Lani shouts, trying to help.

"Sick! Yeahhhh!!" the leader of the pack says.

"Do it some more!!!"

"Duuuhuuude, I'm selling this to girlspuking-dot-com, this is primo shit!"

"Lick it up, dickwad," is about all you can manage in response. Right now, you'd sell your soul for an Evian water and a peppermint Altoid.

"I think you'd better leave the lady alone," a voice demands in a very Superman-like way.

"Fuck off, you fucking Boy Scout!"

You look up and shade your eyes against the blazing sun just in time to see Superman take a swing. He decks the frat-boy with the video camera, sending him stumbling backward.

"*Eagle* Scout," your hero corrects him. He picks up the video camera and pops out the tape, crushing it in one hand like an empty cigarette pack.

"Thank you," you say, as he helps you to an upright position. He's dangerously handsome with take-me-home-to-meet-your-mother eyes. You want to cry as you fling your arms around him. Even Lani joins in the hug, trying ever so subtly to check out his muscled forearms. "Nice," she mouths to you as you let him go.

"I would hate for a girl like you to end up on some website that showcases people's embarrassing moments," the Eagle Scout says.

"You saw me . . . ?" you say, mortified. Everybody knows it's a rule that a guy will never have sex with a girl once he's seen her puke.

"It wasn't that bad," he says, smiling a little longer than he needs to. "I've seen much worse. I volunteer by helping elderly cancer patients through chemotherapy. It sounds corny, but I find that helping people is a rewarding part of my life."

"Gosh. Can we buy you a beer or something? As thanks?" Lani asks.

"Naw, it was nothing."

"Surely there's something we can do to make this up to

you," you say, with cute pouty lips. "And I've never met an Eagle Scout."

"I'll tell you what," he says, "I'm supposed to meet some friends for a boat trip in about a half hour. It's a private yacht, catered food . . . you'd probably think it's kinda boring, but they asked me to invite people."

"I didn't even know there was an ocean near here," you joke lamely. "Can you give us a minute?"

"Take your time," he says. You pull Lani aside.

"Duh. We're going," she says.

"You don't just meet people who ask you to go on yacht trips!"

"We just did."

"What if he wants to sell us into white slavery? Or auction off our livers to the Chinese! Or what if he's really really . . ." you trail off as he bends over to tie his shoe. Nice ass. " . . . my future husband." This could be one boat you don't want to miss.

You've had a day full of upheaval already; the last thing you want to do is go on a three-hour tour with a total stranger. Stay on dry ground and turn to page 81.

Three-hour tour or not, it wouldn't be so bad to be trapped on an uncharted desert isle with this guy. To get on the boat, turn to page 25.

You don't want to take your chances with the border patrol! It's Tijuana drug-deal Round Two!

"Hey," you tell Lani, "let's just talk to that guy, get rid of this stuff, and be done with it."

"Are you serious? You don't know him!"

"Look, we didn't know the pharmacist either, and that worked!"

"Sure, it worked. That's why you have a purse full of crack!"

"Shhh! It's not crack, okay?" you say, "I'm losing my buzz and I will not be able to relax until we do this." This seems to register with Lani, who beckons the waiter over from one of the nearby tables.

"Señor?" you ask the young man, "do you have a minute?" He couldn't be a day over seventeen, and couldn't look less threatening. What were you worried about?

"Yes?" he answers.

"Could you meet me in the alley behind the restaurant in five minutes?" You turn to Lani and wink. Why is she rolling her eyes at you? That's how they do deals in Mexico! It's a cultural thing!

"Um, señorita, there is no alley behind this restaurant." Okay, now you feel like a total idiot. Lani nervously puffs away at a cigarette while you do your best to maintain a professional demeanor.

"Look," you say, trying to sound cool, "you're the one who brought it up."

"Sure. Let me see what you have. Hand it to me under the table."

You reach into your handbag and pull out the sack of drugs, handing it under the table to the waiter. "It will cost you fifty American dollars."

Lani gags and coughs on her smoke. You turn around to give her a pleading look and see a tremendous Mexican man looming behind her wearing a police uniform. The policeman approaches the table, pulls out a set of handcuffs, and slaps them on Lani! Before you can protest, you feel your arms being wrenched behind you and the metal clasps clicking around your wrists! The policeman and the waiter start congratulating each other in Spanish.

"Lani, what the hell is going on?"

"This," Lani answers, "is a drug bust."

The men walk you out the front door and into a beat-up cop car, throwing you in the backseat like a sack of potatoes, locking the doors like you're dangerous felons. You look over at Lani, trying not to break down. You feel tears starting to well up, your throat getting dry. The car pulls away and starts toward what will certainly be a dank, dismal, and dangerous Tijuana prison.

"We are allowed one phone call, right?" Lani asks the cops. Their only response is booming laughter.

The End

You're past all those years of sneaking out after curfew and stealing away for a forbidden cigarette. You'll handle this adult to adult.

"Hello," you say calmly, rising off the bed with feigned dignity and poise. "I'm sorry to have startled you—and I just want to tell you what a sincere pleasure . . ." bad choice of words, you think, considering their soiled bed—"*Privilege* it is to make your acquaintance." They are staring at you blankly. It's not working. "If you would be so kind as to let me gather my things," you say, praying they will leave.

More stares.

"Mommm . . ." Billy Backstreet whines. "You're embarrassing me!"

"Listen," you explain, "it's not what it seems. I am Billy's friend from school—uh—high school. I met him down here and we were walking down the street and all of a sudden, I fell—which is how I lost my clothes. Isn't that right, Billy?" He nods, confused. "Yes," you continue, "little gypsy *boys* were grabbing my clothes and had it not been for the bravery of your son, I could have been raped and left in the gutter by *boys*," you say, pointedly.

"You poor thing!" Mommy Dearest cries. "Of course you can get dressed." The Backstreet family files out of the room and Billy Backstreet gives you a little wink and spank on the ass as he leaves. Pervert.

After you've recovered your clothing and smoothed out your wild post-sex hairdo, you glide into the main room with a smile. "Thank you sooo much, but I really have to be going," you say, glaring at Billy.

"Oh, we'd *never* let you out in that city by yourself! After what you've been through, we shouldn't let you out of our sight!" Mom and Dad are practically body-blocking the door. The little sister smiles at you like you're her long-lost cool friend. Billy bashfully stares at his feet. "You *must* come with us! We're going on a guided tour of the Santa Rosos Pottery Factory in twenty minutes! They let you paint your own mugs and we've been looking forward to it all week, haven't we, Billy?" Mom nudges Billy.

"You couldn't be any safer," Dad adds. "Didn't Billy mention I'm a police officer?" You turn a shade of white as Backstreet Senior whips out a genuine police badge. Any ounce of alcohol that was in your system has instantly drained away. You look at all of them with a harrowing realization: The Backstreet family will be your companions for the remainder of the day. You're going to be spending the rest of your Mexico trip dead sober, on a guided tour of a goddamn pottery factory.

"Are you Billy's girlfriend?" Little Sister Backstreet asks, grinning.

"*Yes,*" you manage. "I am Billy's girlfriend."

You want to kill yourself. But, it beats statutory rape charges . . .

The End

In a town like Tijuana, women need to stick together!

"Thanks for letting us sit with you," one of the girls says. "It's a goddamn war zone out there, you know?"

"I know," you reply. "My ass has been grabbed so much it's like public domain."

"Men are the worst. They fail to realize a sweating warthog in a Corona wife-beater is far from impressive."

"Preach on, sister!" Lani shouts, accidentally dropping the cigarette out of her mouth and nearly lighting her hair on fire. "Hey, what are your names?"

"I'm Happy."

"I'm Bashful."

"I'm sure . . ." Lani answers. "Um, who's up for all-you-can-drink tequila shots?"

"You know we're game for *anything*," Bashful says, with a mischievous grin.

Before you can say "sisterhood," tequila is poured into plastic cups and salt and lime are poised and ready to go. First salt. Bashful winks at you as she slowly licks the salt off her wrist. Then comes the tequila. Just as you girls are ready to shoot in unison, Bashful laces her arm into yours so that you are arm in arm while gulping down the booze. Okay, now comes the lime. You all bite down hard, wincing and shrieking.

"It *is* true," you ramble. "It is so damn *true* that this country has got it all figured out, with siestas and shit. Let's face it. And the food! How many ways can you eat a tortilla? Think about it!" You have no concept of how long you have been waxing poetic. You feel as if you are about to touch on something deeply profound, like it's just within your drunken grasp.

"Would you listen to yourself?" Bashful is saying, "Because you are so fucking on it!"

As you inhale your cigarette, her head is resting on your shoulder, her arm slung around yours. Your world is hazy and amazingly comfortable. Across the club you spot Lani and Happy on the dance floor, mock-grinding each other, creating masturbation fodder for every man in the club. It's quite a show.

"Here," Bashful takes off one of her leather arm cuffs and fastens it around your wrist. "I want you to wear this. Now we're like the Wonder Twins."

"God, thanks."

"Hey," she puts her hand on the back of your neck and starts playing with your hair, "I am really glad we're here."

"Me, too. This is the best damn lunch ever." Is it even still lunchtime?

"No," she says, "I mean I'm glad *we're* here." Her hand is on your bare knee and her black fingernails are tickling the inside of your leg. You turn to face her and your noses are inches away. Her breath smells of menthols and she is giving you fuck-me eyes. You spot Lani and Happy on the dance floor: Happy is behind Lani, slapping her ass, and Lani is bent over laughing. Hmmm . . .

"Look, um, Bashful, I have never, you know, and it's fine if you and Happy are *whatever,* but the thing is this—I am a modern woman, but not that modern."

"No one would ever have to know," she whispers.

Bashful leans in to you and softly kisses your lips. Wow. It feels like kissing a guy, but no stubble. You are exhilarated—this is something you would never do back in the States, let alone in public! She pulls back and smiles at you. You smile back, and then you lean in to her to give her a full kiss. You slide your tongue into her mouth and put your hands on her cheeks. You can feel her hands start to slink around your waist, and you move in closer. Her hands slip up your back, and you can feel her nails slowly stroking you. Suddenly, you feel a third hand, tapping your shoulder. You swing around.

"Oh—I thought that was you!" Oh my god. It's this loud-mouth, Neil, who you dated years ago. "I had a bet with my table that was you! Thanks, you just won me twenty dollars." He leans in closer. "Shit, babe, if I knew you were into this kinky shit, we could have made our relationship work. Fuck! I can't believe you freaked out when I asked you to do a three-way with me and my ex-girlfriend. Just promise you'll keep me in mind when you ladies need a little hard action, if you know what I mean," he says.

"Let's just keep this between us," you plead with him.

"Yeah right," Neil laughs.

"Oh my God," you say, realizing Neil's table is full of vaguely familiar faces.

"Tease," Bashful scolds you, leaving the table. Your stomach sinks. Sometimes what happens in Mexico does not always stay in Mexico.

The End

Running is not an option. It is undignified and you might fuck up your Prada heels.

You march back over to the cockfight bookie to explain why there will be no more money for him today. *"Señor, no dinero!"* you shout. This can't be the first time someone has stiffed him. Its not like he is a legit Vegas sports bookie or something.

The man whistles, and suddenly you are surrounded by four of the hugest Mexican banditos you have ever seen. One of the men places his hands on your shoulders and begins to push you toward the front of the party. Lani trails behind you, trying to reason with the bookie in her worst Spanglish. You cannot be sure, but you think you overhear her offering to show her tits if they let you go.

One of the banditos lifts you up onto the stage next to the bloody chicken-wire arena. Dumbly standing on the stage alone, you scour the crowd for Lani, but she is nowhere to be found, undoubtedly being guarded by the banditos. You secretly hope the bookie took her up on her offer to flash them. A hush falls over the crowd and people begin to stare. Shit, are they expecting you to sing and tap-dance or something?

One of the massive banditos lifts you in the air and drops you inside the cockfighting ring. The ground is covered with a pungent mixture of blood, chicken guts, and feathers. You can see gizzards and entrails hanging on the wire fences surrounding you. You might vomit now, and it's *not* the tequila. With a swoop, the bandito pushes something into you hands. You look down to see what you're holding. It's a mop.

"Oh my God," you scream in horror. "I can't clean!" Your protests are met only with cheers and chants from the audience. You feel like a caged animal, and in fact you are. There is no escape until you clean up the splattered chicken guts. You slosh through the mess with the mop, which really just spreads everything around. As you clean, your feet and Prada shoes become encrusted with feathers and blood. Oh my God, was that a beak? This is how you will spend the rest of your Tijuana adventure, up to your ass in chicken chum.

The End

Becoming a Tequila Queen may be a delusion of grandeur, but it's your delusion. Isn't this how Bill Gates got started?

The taco guy accompanies you to a bank, which is about as user-friendly as one would expect in this little border town. You take a deep breath and withdraw every penny you have in your account. After you hand him the cash, he hands you the tequila recipe. You write his address on the back of the goatskin with a Bic pen, figuring this guy should be compensated if you strike gold. The Taco Bandito—whose real name turns out to be Jesus, appropriately enough—gives you a few words of encouragement in "Spanglish" and disappears in a cloud of spliff smoke. The only thing left now is to call your uncle Shecky, a one-time felon and some-time marijuana grower who has become a rather legit microbrewer in Northern California. With his backing and your tequila formula, you'll be unstoppable. Right?

Lani looks at you disapprovingly. She who maxed out her credit cards last year to buy a bong autographed by Cheech and Chong. "Well," she sighs. "Now that you've sunk your whole future into a tequila formula written on goatskin, wanna head back?"

A year later, *Blood Duel Tequila* is the hottest item to hit liquor stores since boxed wine. You've got a massive house on the ocean with one of those infinity pools where it looks like the water just keeps going. The newspapers call you the Tequila Queen, and you're one of the richest young businesswomen in America, right up there with that girl who started her own nail-polish empire in her dorm room. Lani now has the lifestyle of her dreams. She's the head of *Blood Duel Tequila* public relations; her duties consist of throwing parties and getting people drunk on your product. Uncle Shecky has a piece of the pie too, and his own Humboldt County estate where he hides out, drinks tequila, and studies "horticulture." Even you couldn't have predicted this looking back on your life—after all those classes, teachers, obligations, and lame jobs—all you really needed was a trip to Mexico.

And what, you may ask, became of Jesus, the Taco Bandito? When the money rolled in, you and Lani went back to Tijuana on a pilgrimage to thank him with a suitcase full of cash. But the man was nowhere to be found. He'd vanished without a trace. You have scoured countrysides and spoken to historians, but nobody can find Jesus. Nobody has even heard the story of the blood duel, a tale chronicled on every *Blood Duel Tequila* label. Only Lani believes that Jesus was indeed real, and sometimes even she questions it, reminding you that you were both "fucking lit like a cheap Tijuana firecracker."

You take a sip of your tequila, staring out at the bluest ocean you've ever seen. Sometimes in life you have to take a leap of faith even if it means spending your life savings on a goatskin. Wherever Jesus is now, you hope he's smiling down on you with those creepy teeth, laughing through a cloud of smoke, and cooking God a taco.

The End

Yacht or not, it's always wise to listen to the little voice in your head that reminds you it's easier to go through life with two kidneys instead of one.

"You know what? We're gonna pass," you say with a cute little smile. "I don't think I could deal with getting seasick after my pukey ways."

Lani stands there, awestruck, impressed that you could resist the magical pull of the Eagle Scout. He shakes his head, disappointed. "Well, y'all have a great siesta," he says. "Be careful out there."

"Adios!" Lani shouts after him. She turns to you and angrily lights a cigarette. "What the hell are you doing?"

"I don't know," you say. "I got some sort of weird vibe from him. He may be an Eagle Scout, but I think there's something else going on there."

"Cult member?"

"Or religious."

"Ugh," Lani snorts.

As Lani dwells on this, you notice your Eagle Scout has quickly forgotten all about you. He's helping two moms squeeze limes into their Coronas at an outdoor café across the plaza. Eagle Scout to the rescue. You guess you weren't so special after all. Suddenly, you feel eyes on you. The ground begins to shake, but it's not an earthquake. It's the pitter-patter of little feet.

"Lani . . ." you say as you turn around.

"What the hell!" she screams.

From everywhere, it seems, small children swarm toward you. They're barely even kids, they're *toddlers*. Dozens of them. They jabber at each other in Spanish, excited and smiling. They're not threatening, but there are so many of them! Coming out of stores and alleys and houses and apartments . . . all to stare at you and Lani.

"Back away slowly," you whisper to Lani. You both try your best, but the children move with you. "What do you think they want?"

"I don't know," answers Lani, her voice thick with terror. "Just keep walking." Your pace quickens, but they close in, like the two of you are the queen bees and they're the workers. And they're smiling and laughing, like it's a game. These kids don't know they're scary, which makes them terrifying.

"What . . . is . . . going . . . on!" you say, trying not to step on a really cute little girl. "Why are they laughing?" You shush the kids (this is something that transcends all cultures and is understood by children of any nation). In the distance, you hear a familiar guffaw. You look up to see where the laughter's coming from.

Up on the balcony of some lame-ass club, the video-wielding fratboys are drinking beers and watching you and Lani and your flock of children. They are laughing like this is the funniest thing in the whole world. Each fratboy holds a carton of Chicklets. It dawns on you. These kids are the army of Chicklet children, a common sight in Mexico, and it's their goal to unload as much gum as possible to help support their families. What the hell are they doing following *you* around?

"What the fuck!" you scream at Fratty and the fratboys.

"Duhudde—you shouldn't have messed with our shit," Fratty yells.

"You tried to videotape me vomiting!"

"We made a deal with these kids. We bought all their gum and they're gonna follow you girls all day long!"

"No *way*," Lani says. Then she looks at the kids. They are grinning like freshmen pledges trying to make it into the coolest house on campus.

"You're exploiting these children," you protest.

"Exploit this, bitch!" he shouts back, grabbing his crotch. And with a final laugh, the fratboys disappear into the club. The little kids are having the time of their life. This is much more fun than hawking chewing gum to tourists. They're playing a game and you're "it." You look to Lani. The two of you had planned to go drinking, do a little sightseeing, maybe catch a mariachi band, but now you're going to have to wander around the streets for the rest of your trip, like the Pied Pipers of Tijuana.

"Hey, Lani," you say, "wanna know something funny?"

"*What.*"

"After the taco and the water and the vomiting, I could really use a piece of gum."

The End

The idea of owning a bottle of Viagra would not make your mother proud, so you're gonna go for the Claritin.

"Sorry, Lani. I don't have a penis or a boyfriend with one, so I'm thinking the Viagra's not on my menu for this trip."

"That . . . is . . . soo . . . flaccid of you."

"Señor!" you call to the pharmacist/dealer, "As much Claritin as this will buy!" You slap down a wad of cash that makes him grin. Lani pouts, looking at the menu of drugs she never got to experience.

"This trip sucks donkey," Lani groans. "The only thing I did was buy a bunch of gum from some kids. You'll be sniffle-free for the rest of the year but I'm . . ." her eyes wander to a nearby market stand selling sparkly jeweled purses, completely covered in rhinestones, shaped like everything from Diet Coke cans to Edvard Munch's *The Scream*. "So shiny . . ." she mumbles. You allow Lani to drag you over to the purses. She examines each one, intent on finding one that's suitable for both day and night. She's deciding between a Budweiser bottle one and another that's apparently supposed to be Yoda, when a man appears, as if from nowhere.

"You have met my children," his deep voice booms. You and Lani cling to each other for dear life. He is a giant man who wears a sparkling white suit and matching fedora. You notice his cufflinks are made of small, rounded squares—Chicklets. "I am Don Chicallio. My children call me Don Chicklet. My children say you have been very generous to them."

"*Gracias,*" you manage.

"No. It is I who owe you thanks. You have reignited the spirit of my children, and for that, I would like to have you at my estate this afternoon. I am having a fiesta to celebrate my fiftieth birthday. I told my children they may invite two people. They have chosen you."

"But, we just gave them a few doll—" Lani starts to say before you smack her.

"Don Chicklet, we're flattered by your offer," you say.

With a quick smile to Don Chicklet, Lani pulls you aside. "No way in hell am I going to Don Corleone's birthday party. He's probably into all kinds of crazy shit!"

"He's into chewing gum."

"That's the tip of the iceberg! Look at that guy! He's freaking me out! Let's just buy the purses and jet."

"Lani, do you really want to be the one to say *no* to the man who controls the lucrative Tijuana chewing gum trade? It's his fiftieth birthday!"

If you think that attending Don Chicklet's birthday party is an offer you cannot refuse, turn to page 33.

Maybe this whole thing is a strange ploy to force you to create more Chicklet saleschildren. Politely decline and turn to page 98.

You are not one to be bullied around by a corrupt policeman. You have rights, don't you?

"Dan," you say calmly, "tell the officer to just write me out a ticket for public urination, or whatever inane law I have fractured, and I will take care of it when I return to the States."

"Are you sure? I mean, that's really not the best idea."

"Of course, I'm sure. This is not some rogue nation; we're in a civilized country. Ask for the ticket."

Dan starts chattering in Spanish to the officer, and gesticulating wildly. The officers exchange glances, and chuckle. You take this as a very bad sign. Suddenly you feel like a caged animal. The officers swing open the car doors and wrench you and Dan from the vehicle. Before you can register what is happening, you feel your chest being slammed against the side of the car, your arms being tugged behind you, and handcuffs squeezing your wrists. The officer jerks you around, and forces you to march to his car, pushing you along by the back of your neck.

Inside the backseat of the police car, dizzy and frightened, you glance over at Dan, who is in a shackled heap beside you. He looks like he has just been punched in the mouth, and his face is starting to swell. "Where are you taking us?" You shout to the two officers in the front seat. But you know where you are heading: a dinky and dirty Mexican jail in the middle of nowhere—where no one can hear you scream. "Where are you taking us?" you try again. Their only reply is to peel out of the dirt embankment and onto the highway, kicking up dust behind you.

The End

You have always been a sucker for Latin men—and you could suck on one right now.

You slink over to the Latin man and say softly in his ear, "I am yours for one dance." After a tense pause, he slips his arms around your waist and literally sweeps you off your feet onto the dance floor. Okay, let's face it, he is amazing. The best straight dancing man since John Travolta. He spins you like a top, dips you back and forth, and holds you close. Last time you tried to dance with a guy like this, you ended up flipping backward over a couch and knocking over a table. When the music stops, you pull away from the Latin man panting like a cat in heat. You can barely catch your breath to ask him, "Who *are* you?"

The Latin Dance Machine tilts your chin up and says hotly, "I have many names. My friends call me Domingo. You will call me Diego." You stifle a giggle and nod. Diego or Domingo spins you into his arms and kisses you. Oh my God, you're drowning from all the saliva he plasters on your lips. Christ, how can he lick your chin and nose at the same time? You manage to spin away, and make some dancelike arm movements to hide the fact that you are wiping your face clean. Diego pulls you back again, and whispers in your ear, "I want you. I must lick you all over."

You gag, and say, "Um, pardon, come again?"

"Yes," he whispers, "I will make you come again, and again, and again." You look in wide-eyed shock at Diego, who licks his lips. "Let's go upstairs." You wrack your brain . . . upstairs . . . oh yeah; the top level where the DJ spins and people have sex in the deserted booths. It wouldn't be a crime to receive several minutes of pleasure from this kind stranger. He may be sloppy, but he certainly has gusto. *Me gusta gusto.*

Latin Lickin' Lover is going to have to find another girl to tongue bathe. Say adios and turn to page 151.

You are too hot and bothered, horny and drunk, silly and sloppy to do anything but take Diego up on his offer. Get ready for some hot public displays of affection. Turn to page 157.

You go ahead and fork over the cash for your giant box full of explosives. At least you'll be the star of your next Fourth of July party.

"Damn," Lani sighs, looking at your firepower. "I feel like a kid again. Wanna blow some shit up?"

"Very funny. Let's get drunk on tequila shots and play with loaded guns while we're at it." Unless you find yourself in the middle of a guerilla warfare attack, there is really no point to hauling this stuff around. "I think we should go drop this back at the car," you suggest.

"Sweet. Let's ditch the M-80s so we can do some drinking."

The marketplace is a war zone in itself. Lani is quick to dart around drunken tourists and small children, but you keep thinking of the explosives in your arms and take it slow. It's like one of those war movies where the bomb you're carrying could go off if someone sneezes. You're relieved when you are finally out of the marketplace, heading down the small street where you left the car.

"Are you sure this is the right place?" you ask. You both stare in horror at the dirt field and the familiar dilapidated shack. This is it, alright. But no car. The realization hits you like a ton of bricks.

"Fuck . . . me . . ." Lani says, turning pale.

"The car is *gone,*" you say, stating the obvious.

"But—this is a good neighborhood. I've never had this happen before!"

"Chop shops are a major industry in Tijuana. It's *gone*," you reiterate.

It looks like Lani might just lose it. With tears welling up in her eyes, she reaches into the dirt and finds her little cardboard tree air freshener. She sobs, *"Evergreen Freshness!"*

"Lani! Get a hold of yourself!" You shake her by the shoulders, "We're gonna take care of this. We will find the car."

"Promise?"

"Sure," you lie.

Lani is drying her tears with the air freshener when you notice a young man emerging from the rickety shack. He wears Levis and one of those shiny polyester shirts that went out of style twenty-five years ago. "Lose your car, no?" he says.

"Lose our car, *yes*. Stolen! *Comprende?*" you shoot back.

The guy smiles. One of his teeth has a gold cap on it. "Maybe you and you fren' need my help," he says.

"Look. I think we're just going to report it to the police," you say, trying to smile politely. "But thanks for your concern."

"Policía? They no do nothing. They take car for selves. You no get nothing."

You ignore the creepy guy and look in the distance. You can see a *policía* station. A bunch of guys with badges play dice games in front of it. Not exactly picture of credibility.

"Come on, Lani," you say. Lani slows her pace, looking desperate.

"I find car for you and you fren'," he says. "For price. Pretty girls half off. *Policía* charge more."

"Maybe we should listen to this guy," Lani whispers. "I gotta get my car back—my car is nicer than my apartment!"

You look at your slick new "fren'" with skepticism. There is little doubt in your mind that he is some sort of criminal. Glancing at the police station, there is *no* doubt in your mind that they *are* criminals. You weigh your options: Who is less likely to rob you blind and sell you into white slavery?

If you decide to roll the dice with the dice-rolling policemen, turn to page 120.

If you've always had a problem with authority figures and would rather trust your new fren', turn to page 57.

Screw this, you think, putting down the tequila shot. The crowd lets out a disappointed groan. Your waiter gives you an ashamed look, picks up the glass himself, and downs the shot!

"Eeewwww!" you shriek.

"My God," Lani yells. "He's chewing it up! Ugh!"

"I swear I'm going to have post-traumatic stress disorder if you don't give me a drag of your smoke," you demand. Gratefully puffing away, you shudder at the thought that you could have had a tequila-soaked earthworm floating around in your tummy.

"Excuse me," says a male voice, "I just want you to know that I am glad you didn't swallow that shot."

"Oh yeah?" you turn around to face a very handsome young American guy. With a baby face and the straightest teeth you've ever seen, he's cute enough to be a member of a boy band. He grins, shamelessly flirting with you. This one's a real cutie. *And* he respects women who don't ingest worms for people's amusement. You flirt right back at him. "I thought I was gonna get kicked out of here."

"Then I wouldn't be able to buy you a drink," he says.

"I'll take anything but a tequila shot."

"You got it," he says, as he walks away to the bar.

"Mmmm," Lani smiles "he's easy on the eyes . . ." Yes, indeedy.

Your Backstreet Boy returns laden with beer, chips, and salsa, or the "breakfast of champions" as he calls it. Over "breakfast" you discover that this particular young man is quite charming, polite, and even more important, smitten with you. When he places his hand on your leg, you don't mind.

"Hey, gorgeous," he says. "Dance with me. This is my favorite song."

"'Mambo Number Five' is your favorite song?" you ask, thinking *strike one.*

"Yeah, uh, only 'cause it reminds me of the summer I spent in Monte Carlo." He answers hastily. Hmmm, you think, handsome *and* wealthy . . .

You and Backstreet grind on the dance floor and in your drunken haze you're pretty sure there were some beer-soaked kisses in there too. Backstreet has a name, but you forgot it and are too embarrassed to ask him a third time. You make a mental note to get Lani to ask him later. Where is she by the way?

"Hey," says Backstreet, "this may sound weird, but do you want to go somewhere a little more private? I've got a place where we can cook food, have a few drinks, and I swear we won't have to hear 'Mambo Number Five.'"

You lock eyes. There is no doubt about it. This boy is hot as they come, and you *are* here for a liberating experience. "Someplace quiet, huh?" you say, coyly. "I might feel bad about ditching my friend."

You both spot her across the bar, on top of a rickety table gyrating to the music. "She looks like she can take care of herself. We can always hook up with her later," he says, laying a big lime-tasting kiss on you. You realize it's either time to get busy getting to know this guy in a carnal sense, or ditch him and break his sweet heart.

"I'll be back in a sec," you say, kissing him as you go. Lani looks over at you from her perch, knowing exactly what you're going to say.

"Do him or I will!" She says, way too loudly.

"I think he's got a hotel room or something."

"Even better! I would have done him in a toilet stall if it was convenient!"

You look over at Backstreet standing under the lights, smiling at you. Temptation. You take a deep breath. What's a girl to do?

If you give in to your raging hormones and take Backstreet up on his attractive offer for what is sure to be a good time, turn to page 115.

If you think the day is still young and there may be cuter fish in the sea, you can break his adorable little heart and turn to page 176.

If the van is a rocking, don't bother knocking!

"Let's go," you say urgently, "right now."

"What's the rush?" he asks. You pull him to the table, grab your purse (for your always trusty rainbow condoms), and announce to Lani and Bill that you will be back soon. You practically run out of the marketplace toward what will be known in the future as the Love Van. The Love Van is not much to look at—it's dark blue, old, a little dirty—but it'll do the job. Jesse rips open the sliding door and you climb inside. Every blanket and pillow imaginable has been piled into the back of the Love Van. You flop onto your back, taking off your clothes before he even shuts the door. It's like your skin crawls, itching to be touched. You are the very definition of hot and bothered. Jesse covers you with kisses. Within seconds, you're both completely stripped naked.

What happens next is less like a sexy Hollywood love scene, and more like the Discovery Channel. It is positively carnal and wild. You mount him on top, he flips you under him, you hang from the rafters, you stick your feet out the window, he spins you like a top. His every stroke inside of you produces a powerful rush. It's not like you are going to reach an orgasm, it's like you're already there, riding it through! And then, just when you thought you had felt everything, been to the highest realms of ecstasy, a very intense buzz rises inside of you, you get hotter, wilder, hotter, wilder, and boom! Suddenly you sing out loud, screeching like a banshee, practically out of your body! You have attained a higher consciousness! This must be nirvana! Slowly, you float back down to earth and cuddle next to what's-his-name. You're tingly, feeling like you have just been buffed to a high sheen. You better enjoy this moment now, because you will spend the rest of your life trying to replicate it.

In a few weeks you are no longer able to have sex without Viagra. You crave it so much, you buy bottles of the stuff illegally each month. Although you know your sex drive will be dysfunctional for life, there are benefits to being hooked on Viagra . . . like the road trips you and Lani take to Tijuana in order to get it.

The End

You are having visions of screaming children throwing wads of gum in your hair. Don Chicklet's party is a no-go.

"I am sorry, Don Doublemint, whatever, we already have plans," you say weakly. He looks at you in sadness and dismay, as if no one has ever dared decline an invite to a gum party.

Pangs of guilt rise inside your stomach, and you are just about to accept his offer when Lani tugs on your arm and says, "Oh look, there's a legless street perfomer!" She drags you toward a crowd of people gathering around what might be the worst public performance you have ever witnessed. As you watch the jig, you silently wonder how someone can do the Mexican hat dance without legs. Or a hat. Transfixed by the horrific act, you barely notice the Men In Suits before it is too late.

"Lani," you whisper, freaked. The men are everywhere, closing in on you. They look like FBI. Does Mexico have an FBI?

"Pardon me, miss?" Only asshole guys in authority positions call you "miss" because they know that it's just bullshit courtesy. "We're gonna have to take a look in that bag you're carrying," they say, moving toward you.

"Who the hell are you guys?" you choke, your throat suddenly dry as a bone.

"We work for the United States–Mexico drug import-export pharmaceutical task force."

"Like that exists," Lani mutters.

"Hmm, lookie what we have here," he says, grabbing the shopping bag from your hands. Before you have a chance to scream about illegal search and seizure, he has found your newly purchased Claritin. "You're not planning on bringing that back stateside, are you?"

"No. I live here," you try. "In a tar-paper shack down the road. But I'm allergic to tar-paper, so . . . I need the Claritin."

"Nice story, ladies, but we hear that line every day."

They always go from "miss" to "ladies." The pricks. Who knew the United States pharmaceutical industry had so much pull south of the border! Then again, anybody with fifty cents has pull south of the border. Lani grabs your arm, backing away as the men come at you from all sides.

"Do you know that drug trafficking is a federal offense?" He begins his tirade. "You could land yourself twenty years in the pen . . ." he babbles, full of puffed up machismo, but you can no longer pay attention. You glance over his shoulder to see the statuesque Don Chicklet with his Chicklet children flocked around him. You stare at him pleadingly, imploring him to help. You hear the macho-man say something about "a body cavity search." Don Chicklet locks eyes with you and shakes his head, putting his arms around his flock as he turns and walks away.

The End

You get close to Lani and whisper in her ear, "He's mine. You got the last twelve guys we've met at parties and you OWE me." Lani whimpers just to make you feel bad, and then shakes it off.

"Two Petron margaritas for the prettiest women at the party," Julio says, handing you both frosty glasses rimmed with salt.

"Oh, I bet you say that to all the girls," you coo, glancing around the party. No, he was right—you are definitely the prettiest women at the party.

"Uhhh—look. I'm gonna go check out the stables or something," Lani says in a half-assed lie. With a dejected sigh, Lani heads off through the party. Julio takes your free hand and leads you onto the dance floor. The DJ thankfully stops spinning international party hits, and a mariachi musician comes on stage. He plays some soulful Latin melody as Julio holds you close. You realize there must not be an ounce of fat on this guy. He is *cut*.

"I would like to know everything about you," Julio whispers. "You are a mystery to me. There is nothing a man likes more than solving the great mystery that is a beautiful woman."

This guy really knows how to talk. The last dance-floor conversation you had involved some asshole explaining that only losers try to mix Jagermeister since it should really just be taken straight. This is quite a change. You launch into your life story, complete with family scandals and lost loves, and Julio actually listens. As for Julio's life story, he is a student on his way to becoming a pediatrician. He loves kids. He reads poetry in Spanish and English. He is *perfect*. You both even have the same favorite movie, *Like Water for Chocolate*. Actually, you don't tell him you count this as your favorite foreign film, because he wouldn't be as impressed if you admitted your favorite movie was *Dirty Dancing*.

"I could dance with you all night," you tell him.

"I would like to keep you here with me in Mexico, and make sure you never need a single thing ever again," Julio says. "Let me make you happy." A little tear escapes from your eye.

You tilt your face up, and soon you are kissing Julio in the middle of the dance floor. The sun is setting, giving the sky a purplish glow. You never believed it when people in love talked about how it felt like they were floating, but now you know it is true. You and Julio don't spend all night on the dance floor, however. At your request, he leads you to his villa on the estate. After a night of the most intense and passionate love-making you have ever experienced, you want nothing more in life than to be Mrs. Julio Whatever-His-Last-Name-Is.

Six months later, Don Chicklet has once again thrown a massive party at his estate. Why? You are now the blushing bride. Mrs. Julio! You're wearing a white (Lani laughed about that for a long time) Vera Wang dress and Julio's wearing a tux by Armani. You even have those little white and yellow roses in your hair like you've dreamed of since you were eight years old. The best part is that the Chicklet children who first brought you here are the flower girls and ring bearers, and it's the most adorable thing you could imagine.

You and Julio take the dance floor for the first time as a married couple, in the exact same spot where you had your first kiss. As the music pours across the dance floor, you look up at Julio and swear you can see your future in his eyes. Even Lani is happy for you, because she's now dating Julio's younger brother Juan, who hopes to become a politician and help the underprivileged of Mexico get back on their feet. Lani thinks that means she's gonna be "princess of Mexico or something, right?"

"Julio," you say with a smile. "Did you ever think it would end up like this?"

"Only the very moment I saw you," Julio says, kissing you tenderly.

The End

You only live once—participating in an exploitive dance competition is no crime. Besides, you figure, would Madonna do it? Hell, yes!

"I'm going for it," you scream, scrambling from the table. "Hold my purse!"

"Did you ever know that you're my hero?" Lani says solemnly.

"Just make sure there's a cold one waiting for my triumphant return," you say, before scampering off. You push your way through the crowd of men gathering around the stage. Your heart starts to pound, that nervous feeling reminiscent of the time you were sent to the principal's office, something like butterflies and shame and exhilaration.

On stage, spotlights blind you. You take a deep breath and repeat your new mantra: "It's Mexico. Only Mexico." This statement is somehow calming and profound in your drunken stupor. The DJ starts pumping lame MTV spring-break electronica. Shit. Why couldn't they play something more bump and grind?

All the girls standing next to you wriggle and sway with the music, and a man wearing a sombrero and a "No Fat Chicks" T-shirt wanders around the stage tapping girls and dismissing them. You close your eyes and let it all go. In your margarita haze, you're pretty sure you're freakin' like Paula Abdul in a Lakers-girl routine. You shake your thang like something out of a rap video, and even grab your crotch in homage to Madonna, The Great One. So caught up are you in your dance spectacular, you barely notice that the audience has been drenching you with Super Soakers.

You feel a surge of excitement. It's come down to you and one other woman. You might actually win this thing! Sizing up the competition, you realize there is no contest. The woman next to you is about ten years older, fifteen pounds heavier, and dressed head to toe in TJ Maxx. Still, victory must be assured. You face the audience, take a deep breath, and flash your tits. The music screeches to a stop. The crowd roars. The announcer piles gifts and prizes into your arms! You've won!

Back at the table, you share a pitcher of margaritas with Lani and bask in the afterglow. Parked between the two of you is the new man in your life, the Homer Simpson piñata. Lani has even managed to dangle a cigarette from his smiling lips.

"We have $250, and the day is still young," you say, handing Lani the envelope full of cash. "I say we go shopping—with that kind of cash we could probably buy a nice piece of property."

"Hello, ladies," says a handsome and very clean-cut American man who has dared to approach your table. "I was wondering if I could buy you a drink."

Lani gags on her margarita, "Don't you think we've had enough? I mean, you saw her performance up there!"

You smack Lani and turn to the guy. "As you can see, we already have a male companion with us. We don't want to offend Señor Homer."

"That's too bad," he answers. "My associates and I would really love it if you joined us."

You look over his shoulder and see a table of about half a

dozen men that look like they have been ripped from the pages of the Abercrombie & Fitch catalog. They are all gorgeous—and wearing polo shirts and shit. You and Lani exchange knowing glances. These men are ripe and corruptible. Yum.

"Why don't you give us moment?" you ask, and he politely moves away. "Lani, these men are adorable. I bet they have Southern accents!"

"As much as I would love to be in a fratboy sandwich, how long are we really going to sit here at Café Pacific? Let's go spend some of your prize money and see where the day takes us."

She has a point. Would you rather spend your day getting acquainted with a table of beautiful hunks (who probably bleach their teeth and do weekly facial masks) or breathing in some fresh Tijuana air while *shopping* with your free money? If only you had to face such harsh choices every day . . .

You're a sucker for a pretty face, and you wouldn't mind sucking on a pretty face. Go and sit with the boys and turn to page 138.

Shopping is your true companion! Go spend your hard-earned striptease money and turn to page 154.

You would rather make a run for it than trust a grubby little bus-boy. Congratulations, you have graduated into international drug smuggling.

"I don't care how, but we can get this over the border ourselves. Let's *vámonos*," you say, as you leave the taqueria.

"Now where did I park my baby?" Lani looks around and lights her fiftieth cigarette of the day.

"If I remember, we take a left at the rabid dog, continue along the gutter full of piss, and hang a right where the street whores are shooting up."

"Hey, it was free." Lani looks at you and smiles. "Wait—I am about to be totally brilliant."

"Let me guess—we smoke all the weed now so there will be no evidence?"

"No, I mean, I am so James Bond." She grabs your arm and drags you to a few deserted tables and chairs near a closed coffee shop, sitting you down at a small, shaded table.

"Give me the weed," she says, as she places the Homer Simpson piñata you won at Café Pacific on her lap. "We are about to give Homer the enema of a lifetime."

Your eyes widen and you begin to understand. "I swear, if I did not know better, I would say you had done this before." You hand the bag of weed—and the mystery powder—to her under the table.

Lani takes her car keys out. "Sorry, Homer" she says, stabbing the longest and most menacing looking key between the piñata's legs. She moves the key dangerously close to the Simpson family jewels.

"Will you cut it out before we get arrested for the inappropriate use of a children's party toy?"

She takes the rolled-up baggie and slips it right into Homer's newly formed hiding spot. Brilliant. "Now," she says, as you start walking to the car, "if we get caught we will cry, give them money, make out with them, whatever. Just don't wind up in prison, 'cause you will be eaten alive. I once knew this girl . . ."

"A friend of a friend," you say. "Believe me, I am NOT going to be 'this girl.'"

It's amazing that Lani's car is still where you left it, because in your opinion, you parked on someone's front lawn. You climb in the Mad Max Mobile and place Homer between the two of you on the front seat. Lani revs the engine, kicks up some dust, and peels into the street. You light up your final menthol like you are about to face the firing squad. Lani plucks the cigarette from your mouth and throws it out the window. "Not at the border," she says, all business. "They'll assume you're a kid who's too drunk to drive and trying to hide it."

"Um," you say, "hate to point this out to you, but we are too drunk to drive."

"Just be cool. They can smell fear." Lani flips on the radio and plays "Easy Like Sunday Morning" by Lionel Ritchie. If Lionel can't mellow you, no one can. You are in a slow-moving line of cars that are going through the border crossing. Ahead of you is a giant sign that marks the border reading "Entering United States." You can feel your heart creeping up your throat.

"Easy like Sunday morning . . ." Lani sings. She squeezes your knee and gives you a reassuring smile. You are one car away. You see that a wrinkled old lady in an official uniform is checking the cars in your lane. Shit, why couldn't you get the male border patrol? The car inches up to what looks like a toll-booth. You hold your breath and try not to fidget. The woman bends over to peer in the car, and you try to look at her in the most nonsmiling, nonsuspicious, nonthreatening, and non-bitchy way. The result is the look of stone-cold fear. She looks at you, Homer, and Lani, then stands up and waves you through!

You drive away in silence. Over to your right you see cars that have been pulled over with orange numbered pylons placed on the roofs. The unfortunate cars are literally torn apart by *Federales*, and the people milling around them are hopelessly despondent. You look ahead at the open road. "Let's have a party," you propose. "You bring Homer and the tequila, and I'll bring my druggie cousin. He can tell us exactly what that white shit is."

"I didn't know your cousin was a druggie."

"He's a pharmacology student. Which is kind of like the same thing."

You giggle and give Homer a kiss. Lani yells, *"Olé! Arriba!"* She guns the car and races up the highway.

The End

You are excited to take your first foray into police bribery. Besides, Lani looks suicidally depressed and you would do anything to find her car.

"Alright," you grumble, digging through your purse. "I'll give you your fifty stinking dollars. But I just want you to know that this kind of police corruption would never happen in the United States." You hand over the fifty bucks to the policeman. He inspects the bill and pockets it, turning to you and Lani. "Okay, you follow me." He says, heading down a residential street. You and Lani trot behind him.

"See?" you say to Lani in an attempt to cheer her up, "See? The car was probably just impounded or towed and he knows where it is." Lani's still shell-shocked, and doesn't seem to understand anything you're saying. Her lips are moving slightly. When you listen closely, you hear that she's just muttering, "Please be alive, please be alive," over and over again, as if to send a telepathic message to her missing car. She's in a bad way.

After a healthy walk, the policeman has led you to an industrial side of town. Houses and yards mingle with abandoned warehouses and overflowing junkyards. The officer heads toward an abandoned gas station, and tells you to wait by the rusting gas pumps while he goes around back. It occurs to you that you could potentially be in grave danger, because this officer is clearly corrupt and has led you to a nasty neighborhood where no one can hear you scream. You don't share this fear with Lani. She's practically catatonic and humming to herself, like Ophelia in *Hamlet* before she goes batshit crazy.

"You gonna be okay?" you ask her, cautiously.

"I wrote a song. In my head. It's about my car. Do you want to hear it?" Lani says, expressionless. Okay, it's official; your best friend has cracked.

A rumbling noise emerges from the gas station garage, startling you. The door slowly rises open, and like some amazing magic trick, Lani's car is inside! But something's off. It has become the latest victim of this Mexican chop shop. It is now painted a metallic grape purple, with a gold lightning bolt painted down the side. On the hood of the car is an airbrushed scene of a phoenix rising from the ashes. The rims, bumpers, and hubcaps are now plated with fake gold. Inside, the dashboard, steering wheel, and car seats have been reupholstered in thick red shag. A miniature Mexican flag flies from the radio antenna. The police officer climbs into the front seat and says, "Check this out!" The entire car starts hopping up and down like an old-school rap video, and the horn joyously sings "La Cucaracha."

"My car," Lani whispers, snapping out of it. You brace yourself, wondering if she will freak out. "I totally love it!" She gets into the car and ceremoniously hangs the evergreen air freshener on her new chrome rearview mirror, tears of joy running down her cheeks.

The End

You've seen enough illegal substances today. You're taking the ride back to Tijuana.

Once you finally drag Lani away from Surfer Shane, you hit the road. The nice gentleman whose Volkswagen microbus you're traveling in tells you his name is Chad and that his "big mama" is having a birthday party in San Diego that he cannot miss. What a sweet guy. He even lets you pick the music as you ride north. Dizzy from the sun, you and Lani fall into a light sleep in the backseat to the sound of the Grateful Dead.

You wake up an hour or two later. The VW's motor's running but Chad is nowhere to be found. You think you've gone blind, but it's only those bright flashlights shining in your eyes.

"What the hell's going on?" you mutter, sleepily.

"We're at the border," Lani says, looking out the window. She's right. The VW sits in a long line of cars, holding up traffic. For some odd reason, Chad has bolted. He didn't even take his keys with him.

A United States customs agent has uncovered something in the back of the microbus. It looks like about one hundred sheets of paper, each with cute Deadhead bears on it in a pattern. "Ladies," the agent says, "you've got some explaining to do."

"Hey, it's Grateful Dead wrapping paper," Lani says.

"I don't care if you're the driver or not, somebody's gotta answer for this. You've got enough hallucinogens here to send you both away for a long time."

"But it's not ours!" you plead.

"Kid, if I had a nickel for every time one of you punks used that line, I'd be a multi-freakin'-millionaire," the customs guy says. You look to Lani. She looks terrified. She should be. You two have just been busted for drug trafficking.

"What a long, strange trip it's been," you try. You and Lani laugh, but it's the last happy moment you'll have for the next few humiliating months. Soon your days will be spent wearing an orange vest, picking up trash on the side of the highway.

The End

Purple Haze is running through your brain—so light up and puff away!

Intrigued by the furry purple-haired marijuana, you bid your ride a safe trip back to the States and sit next to your scruffy friend. Lani and Shane take a seat next to you, forming a circle in the sand. With the excitement of a kid on Christmas morning, you open up the sack of weed, inhale the intense woody aroma, and pinch off a few sticky buds. It is your honor to pack the pipe, which you do with the caution and care you would use to handle a baby bird. The "weed man" hands you a lighter and asks you to start the festivities.

You spark the bowl and inhale deeply. The smoke is dark and heavy, and it enters your lungs so quickly that you have to gag and cough. You cough so hard that little tears drip out of the corners of your eyes, and soon your hacking turns to laughter. You hand the pipe around the circle once. And again. You lean back on your hands and look up at the sky. The sun is getting lower, and everything is awash in a golden glow. Above, palm fronds blow in the wind, and the waves crash against the shore. You have never felt so relaxed and happy, blessed to be in such a beautiful place with such great people. Not to mention this wonderful, magical weed. The last thing you remember is watching the clouds morph into wild fluid images.

When you open your eyes, the sun looks strangely different. Now it's behind the trees, not over the ocean. You glance around and see that the beach is deserted. The fire pit is now a pile of smoldering ash. You try to sit up but you feel a pain in your side so sharp and jagged that you let out a little yelp. You expect Lani to come running, but she is nowhere to be found. It feels like your appendix has burst, and you are nauseous from the pain. Though you are light-headed, you manage to focus and can see that there is a disturbing ten-inch slashing wound on the right side of your belly. The raw cut looks like it's been sewn up with clear plastic fishing wire. Ugh, you wish you hadn't seen that, now you feel sicker. As you hyperventilate, you figure out what has happened. You are no longer in possession of all of your organs. Somewhere out there, your kidney is on the black market.

The End

Okay, you may have found the love of your life (at least for tonight) and you are ready to seal the deal. You've gone back to Backstreet's place and left the crowded sweaty masses behind.

"Wow, this is a really nice place," you say, looking at the huge condo you've just walked into. The terra cotta floors, the hurricane fans, the ocean view, the general cleanliness of the place . . . it hardly seems like you're in Tijuana anymore.

"Thanks. It's costing me a bundle, but it's worth every penny. I like to keep a place down here so I can get away from time to time. You'd be surprised how peaceful it can be," he says, opening the windows and letting in a cool breeze.

You stare out the French doors at the ocean far in the distance, trying to ignore the screams of the feral cats below. Backstreet slides an arm around you. He's not going to let this conversation drone on and on. Thank God, you think. You absolutely hate nervous guys—it reminds you of high-school dances and sweaty palms. There is nothing immature about this boy. You *scored*.

He kisses the back of your neck. You spin around and meet his lips that taste of cheap tequila and Coronitas. It's been so long since you've experienced such a powerful kisser. It's not long before both of you stagger toward the bed in a tangled embrace. You collapse on the four-poster bed, but quickly realize there is something jamming into your back. It's a sightseeing book the size of a small dictionary. You toss it on the floor and get back into the groove.

"I think we should get out of these uncomfortable clothes," you whisper in his ear. He grins and sits up, tearing off his T-shirt. "Are you a swimmer?" you ask as you drag your hands across his completely hairless chest.

"Um, yeah, whatever," he replies as you fall together again. You continue to kiss and before you know it, you are two lovely, naked people exploring each other's bodies to the fullest extent of the law. You have never felt so sexy and liberated and free. You are the ultimate modern woman!

The best part is, Backstreet keeps asking you what to do. He seems to have an unbridled energy to learn about what gets you off. The only downside is after every climax he asks you, "Did you come? Really? How many is that now?" *Strike two.* You tell yourself this is not a big deal—you're lucky to have found such an attentive lover. You're right in the middle of the throes of passion (for the fourth time, because yes, you are keeping count) when you hear keys in the door.

"Oh, God—oh?!"

"Uh—it's nothing," he says, nuzzling your neck. But the door opens.

"Go away! No maid service!" you yell over your shoulder. You hope whoever it is will be able to leap over that language barrier and get the hell out.

"Billy?" a shrill voice calls out.

"Is that your *girlfriend*?" you whisper, thinking she must be an older woman. Oh my God, you wonder, am I gonna have to hide under the bed? Backstreet pulls away from you, red faced.

"No," he says, barely a whisper. "She's not my girlfriend,"

"*William Donald Danielson Junior! What in God's good name is going on here?*"

You see his terrified eyes. You know what he's going to say before he says it.

"That's my mother."

"How old are you?" you squeak.

"Sixteen. But I'll be seventeen in a month . . ." *Strike three!*

Wrapping a sheet around yourself, you try not to panic. You have just legally raped this naked young man. You spin around to see Billy Backstreet's mother standing in the doorway.

"What are you doing in our bed?" barks a fiftyish man wearing a plaid shirt and a sunburn. There's no question: this is Dad. Just when it couldn't get worse—a little girl's head pokes around the corner with frightened curiosity. This is not how you wanted to meet the family. In emergency adrenaline mode you scan the floor. Purse and sundress are easily within grasp. Shoes are questionable. Underwear? Probably lost forever. You could make a run for it and grab what you can on your way out the door, or stay and face the consequences. It's been a long time since you have been punished by parentals, and you really don't relish getting grounded or whatever the hell these people would do to you. You could just bolt and leave this mess behind. On the other hand, you are an *adult*! You could stay and calmly explain the situation, get dressed, and leave with your dignity and both shoes. Oh shit—little sister is walking in the room—what are you going to do?

If you shove the lil' tyke out of the way, grab your clothes, and run, turn to page 118.

If you decide to wrap your naked body in a sheet and level with these fine, reasonable adults, turn to page 72.

Life is too short for explanations like, "I molested your nubile young son." It's time to make a run for it.

Fueled by a jolt of adrenaline, you spring out of bed and wrap the sheet around you in one swift motion. You dive for your dress and dash across the room for your purse.

"Where in the hell do you think you're going, young lady?" Mommy Dearest screams.

"Come back! What's your number?" your teen lover whines.

You only have one thing on your mind—escape. You practically mow over the little sister as you dash for the front door. You race down the hallway and leap down the stairs, too embarrassed to turn back to the nightmare behind you. You are halfway down the street before you realize you are on a public sidewalk in Tijuana wrapped in a bedsheet with your clothes in your hands. You scurry into an alley around the side of a building, hoping for some privacy. A diseased rooster pecks at your bare toes and you shoo him out of the way. This is your alley, dammit! Looking around furtively, you manage to slip the remainder of your clothes on. But God, if there was ever a town where you didn't want to lose your shoes. They were Prada, you think, choking back tears.

Reminded of the poor refugees in the Balkans, you tear the bedsheet with your teeth (and it's not as easy as it looks in the movies) and wrap the pieces into some sick bastardization of footwear. You shuffle about twenty yards into the street, but the fabric on your feet is slipping. You're desperate. You look around. A taqueria, a zombie dog, that diseased rooster . . . not too many options. Then you hear a tiny voice behind you.

"Zapatos?" You turn to see a little boy.

"Sah-what?" you say, wondering if this is some veiled insult.

"Zapatos!" he says, pointing at your swathed feet.

"Yeah, kid. I know. I certainly don't need to hear it from you." He grabs you by the wrist and leads you down the street. "Where are we going? Where?" you yell, "English? Hello? *Hola?*"

You round the corner with your newfound friend to find a card table with a dozen pairs of crudely made clog-sandals; scraps of pleather, wicker, and cornhusk held together by rusty staples and painted with cow blood. It's the most horrifying footwear you've ever seen.

"Zapatos," the boy proudly says.

"How much?" you gulp at the prospect of purchasing the shoes of Satan.

"Fifty American dollars," he answers with a smile.

You have no choice. The little bastard is going to make a killing off of your misfortune. Shuddering, you hand him the money and take a pair of shoes that looks least likely to give you gangrene. As you wedge the clogs on your feet you realize you have hit an all-time low. Not only are you guilty of statutory rape, but you are committing a far greater crime against fashionable footwear everywhere. You hobble off to find Lani and solace in the bottom of a margarita glass.

The End

Despite horror stories of the "Federales," they must be more trustworthy than a shack-dwelling local. Could it hurt to ask?

"Come on," you say, as you drag Lani away from the crime scene. "We are going to the police."

Lani follows you stiffly as you walk toward the police station with calm determination. Pausing only to shove a cigarette in Lani's frowning mouth, you march up to the impromptu craps game happening in front of the police station.

"Ahem," you purposely clear your throat. "We need your assistance, *por favor.*" There is only a vague recognition of your presence. All eyes are on the dice. *"Excuse me,"* you try again. You step into the craps game just as the dice are rolling and manage to catch one that rolls over your strappy sandals and manicured toenails. Five astounded policemen look up at you. Now you have their attention.

"Hello. I am an American. One of your neighbors from the north. *I need help.*"

All five men rise to their feet and begin to chatter in Spanish. You smile at them blankly and try to look like you're really help-less but not gullible. One of the policemen emerges from the pack.

"What can we do for the American girls?" he asks slowly.

"Our car was stolen," you say. "It was parked right over there in that lot, I mean *right in front of your police station,* and now it's gone."

More Spanish gibberish ensues. As you glance over your shoulder to give Lani a reassuring wink, you notice her long-ingly caressing her evergreen air freshener. She is worse off than you thought.

"Look," the *Federal* says. "Maybe I can help you, maybe not. The one thing I DO know is that you just cost me fifty bucks by walking into my game." He is staring right at you. Shit. "Fifty American dollars would make it up to me, otherwise, I can tell you where to catch the bus back to the United States . . ."

Oh, God—this is too typical. He is clearly soliciting a bribe! In front of his colleagues! "Could you excuse us for one minute?" you say, grabbing Lani. "He wants fifty bucks. Maybe it's worth a try. What do you think?"

"I pay more than fifty bucks in parking tickets in any given month for that car!" Lani says urgently. "Let's just do it!"

"OK, but here's the other thing. I've heard about these scams. We give him cash, and then one of his buddies right next to him arrests us for bribery! I swear. I knew this girl, and that's what happened to her cousin's friend. She had to spend the night in a really gross prison."

"I'm just going to run into traffic now and put myself out of my misery," Lani says, matter-of-factly.

This may be your best chance at finding the car, but you're unfamiliar with the etiquette involving the local custom of bribing policemen. Maybe you should march into the police station and file a report and not deal with this asshole . . .

Do you ignore this policeman with an obvious gambling addiction and try to find someone else to appeal to? Turn to page 178.

Want to participate in the national pastime of police bribery? Turn to page 109.

It's not easy being green, but you're up to the task!

You reach for the lime margarita and suck a healthy slug of the icy drink through a straw. If your little blue pal is lurking somewhere in the drink, you sure as hell can't taste it. You take another sip and relax. Lani and Bill smile deviously. Ugh. Who drugs their friends for sport?

You turn to Jesse and ask him about his reptile collection. As he explains it down to every last iguana, you try to look interested. "Is this boring?" he asks.

"No, I find it fascinating," you lie, trying to focus on his positive attributes, like his green eyes. It's probably the gallons of tequila you have consumed today, but he is starting to look very attractive . . . Jesse takes out a pack of cigarettes, American Spirits. "Oh, my God," you gush, "Those are my third favorite kind of cigarettes!" He flashes you that goofy smile. The two of you are a match made in heaven.

On the edge of the square, a mariachi band plays an upbeat song, and all the drunken American tourists rise from their tables and start to dance. The sun is high and your buzz is strong, so you grab Jesse by the arm and pull him off his chair. As you start to cha-cha-cha away, Lani gives you a little wink.

As you and Jesse sway to the beat, you feel a wave of sexiness, an animalistic hormonal rush. You need Jesse. His arms, his legs, his neck, and everything in between. You grab the back of his head, and pull him into you, planting a big wet kiss on his lips. At first he seems scared of your aggressiveness, but he gets over it quickly. Mmmmm, he tastes like strawberries and nicotine. This is the best kiss you've ever had, and believe it, you've had a lot. Now, you're a young, liberated woman with certain needs. And right now those needs must be fulfilled. "Let's go somewhere," you whisper. "I want you inside of me." Did you say that?

"Okay," Jesse pants, "I've got my van parked around the corner."

You are so pleased that he didn't run away screaming after your pornographic come on that you almost missed the word "*van*." Van? Are you so horny that you are going to screw some guy in the back of a van? You look back to your empty margarita glass and know the amorous longings for this lizard-kid are all phony. But then again, who cares? Didn't you come down here for scandal? Adventure? Sleaze? Besides, if someone doesn't tend to your sexual needs very soon, you may spontaneously combust.

You are dangerously horny, and action must be taken. Get some backseat loving and turn to page 96.

You are not going be the chick that once got boned in a van. Resist the power of the little blue pill! Turn to page 127.

You have decided that you would prefer your first meal in Mexico to come from a place with a roof. Kiss the stoned taco chef adios, you're going to Café Pacific!

Pulling Lani away from the taco shack, you explain that it's not that you don't trust her—you just have a sensitive stomach. Besides, it did not look like the fat chef manning the grill was cooking anything that resembled chicken or beef. Good Christ, what could it have been? Goat? Tongue? Goat tongue?

"Darling," you say, letting her have your last cigarette, "I will make this up to you. I will buy you as many two-dollar margaritas as you can choke down."

"That was my problem the last time I went to Café Pacific."

"What are the chances of you puking drunkenly twice in the same establishment? That's like lightning striking twice or something . . ."

"Fine—you're right. But if I puke, it's *your* strappy sandals that are at risk."

Down the street you see a huge sign that reads "Café Pacific" in 1980's-style pastels. The unmistakable tune of "Who Let the Dogs Out" pumps from inside. Now this could be a problem. Before you walk toward the massive bouncer checking IDs at the door, you deliver a pep talk to Lani. "Look, if it's terrible we will leave. If there are creepy men, we will leave. If they play any Sir Mix-a-Lot songs, we will leave, but we will bravely march into this establishment and get drunk as hell."

She can't help it. She smiles and says, "Aye, Captain."

You enter the club and are immediately confronted by people gyrating on the dance floor, tables, and aisles. You wonder what the hell these folks had for breakfast. It's barely noon.

Lani gets comfortable in a booth while you give your order to a woman in a low-cut top and hot pants. Classy. Despite the language barrier, you manage to order four enchiladas, a bucket of Coronas, four margaritas (two with salt, two without), a pack of Marlboro reds, and two bright pink mystery shots that come in test tubes. "Brunch," Lani grins devilishly as the bounty is laid out before you.

"A toast," you say. "To having the best time we will never, ever remember!"

Liquid brunch begins. Is it you, or does everything taste better in Mexico? They seem to have perfected margaritas, blending the ice, tequila, and lime down to a scientific equation. And the beer is as refreshing as Gatorade might be to someone who actually exercises. Even the mystery test tube shot is tasty. The food? Well, if it were not for the greasy enchiladas, you would certainly be dead from alcohol poisoning.

"Oh my god!!! I *love* this song!" you shriek as the DJ cues up the next tune. You begin to gyrate wildly on the booth. "This is the best fucking *song*!"

"What?" Lani screams, "I thought you hated the 'Thong Song!'"

"Hell no!!! This is my *jam*!!!" Damn. You are an amazing dancer. You are all over the place! You're dancing on the table and spilling drinks. You feel like a sexy goddess! A goddess among mere mortals!

"Attention all *ladies,* we have a very important announcement," the DJ says, fading the music out. "It's time for our dance contest! The winner gets $250, all the tequila you can drink here at Café Pacific, and a Homer Simpson piñata!"

"You should do it!" Lani yells. "You are like, 'Solid Gold' dancer right now! There is no competition out there! Do it!"

"Really? They're going to spray me with hoses and shit. I mean, this dress is dry-clean only."

"Oh my god, I am so sure—wet T-shirt is so early 90s. It's all about who the hottest chick is! It's like that gladiator movie—if the crowd thinks you're hot, then you win!"

"You're kind of right, but I mean, does this mean I can't be a feminist?"

"Honey—nothing that happens in Mexico leaves Mexico, okay?"

Either you're wasted or she's making a really good point. This could be your only chance to enter a shady, drunken dance contest in a foreign country. But what if you *lose*? How humiliating. To be defeated by another drunken skank! There is little time and one tequila shot left on the table for liquid courage . . .

If you decide to be a dancing queen and potentially risk humiliation and a soaked dress for a cheap thrill, turn to page 103.

If you prefer to remain a private dancer and stay at the table, turn to page 129.

You are not going to be another notch on this guy's steering wheel. Say "no thanks" to the van-bang.

You take a deep breath and say, "You know, maybe it's not such a great idea."

He pulls away from you, glaring like you just killed his pet gecko. "What the hell? You are the worst tease I've ever met!" he yells. You try to calm him, but his rant continues. "You practically *beg* me to nail you, and now you're above it all? Fuck this." He storms away, pouting. Geez, what a temper.

You are standing alone in the crowded plaza, grateful you didn't screw a guy with such volatile emotional problems, when you feel a little tingle from deep inside. It almost feels like you have to sneeze, but the sensation is coming from your crotch. The feeling grows and envelops you and runs through your whole body, and suddenly you feel wracked with ecstasy. And then it's over. "What in the fuck was that?" you say out loud. You could be mistaken, but you could swear you just had an orgasm. Standing alone, right in the middle of the market square.

You glance over to your empty margarita glass. There are very dangerous powers at work here. Suddenly, you feel the tingle again, just like the last one, rising from your crotch. Oh shit, this is going to be a big one . . . With the speed and strength of a powerful sneeze, you convulse, and have another orgasm! Sweating and flushed, you look around the square. People are starting to stare. You need to get out of sight. You don't want to be some sideshow freak—Orgasm Girl.

You run for the ladies' room and lock yourself in a stall, just in time for an even stronger orgasm. You wonder if these are like labor pains, getting bigger and more frequent until something cataclysmic occurs. You sit on the back of the toilet tank and light a cigarette. Now you know you've just come, because the smoke tastes damn good.

Fifteen minutes and six orgasms later, you hear Lani entering the bathroom asking if you are puking, and if you need someone to hold back your hair. "I'm fine," you yell from the stall, reluctant to give Lani the satisfaction of knowing her stupid little Viagra game has made you into a hormonal freak.

"Can I get you anything?" Lani yells through the door.

As long as you are stuck here, you may as well make the most of it. "Yeah, margarita on the rocks with salt."

"Okay, rocks, salt . . ."

"Yeah," you say, "and this time, no Viagra."

The End

You have decided to stay dry and play it cool. Wet T-shirt contests are so passé. Would Madonna do it? You think not.

"No way José!" you yell across the bottle-strewn table, "I am going to have to puss out of this one."

"Are you crazy?" Lani yells back, "Do you know what $250 could buy in this town? We could buy our own *farmacia* and retire!"

"So *you* go win it."

Her mouth twists into a grin. "Okay . . . I will." She rips off her sweater, takes her hair down, gulps down the final tequila shot, and bolts toward the stage. She scales the side of the stage just in time to have a giant "9" sign taped to her leg. The DJ starts spinning some euro techno crap and pretty soon the dozen women on the stage are jumping up and down like little bunnies, waving their arms above their heads and squealing in mock-embarrassment. Every girl's face has the same "Oh my God—I can't *believe* I'm doing this" expression. Everyone except Lani. She plays to the crowd like a pro, high-fiving men, flirting with the audience, hiking up her skirt, and working the stage like a rock star.

About five minutes into this spectacle, loaded water guns materialize in the crowd. At the first sign of the water, most of the dancers shriek and leap off the stage in horror, somehow trying to protect their dignity. On the other end of the spectrum is Lani. She marches up to a guy with a squirt gun, grabs it out of his hands, and walks away. She turns to one of the remaining girls, strikes a *Charlie's Angels* pose, and squirts her directly in the ass, sending her marching off the stage. The crowd hoots in approval. Then, Lani pulls a man out of the crowd, pretending to freak him before taking aim with the water gun, firing directly at his crotch. The audience screams wildly. Now Lani and a blonde wearing the number "6" are the only two left. Lani strolls over to her, rips the number off her leg, and tapes it to her own. She stands in the middle of the stage with a giant "69" on her legs, and fires the water gun at the audience. The contest is over. The winner is clear.

"Yeah Laaanii!" You scream, jumping up and down at your booth. "That's my girl," you shriek, "that's my friend!"

Lani bounces back to you with her arms full of prizes: an envelope full of cash, the squirt gun, and a huge Homer Simpson piñata!

"This calls for a victory shot! *Olé!*" You shout, toasting with the cheap tequila. Funny how the taste has mellowed in the past few hours.

Two leggy girls approach your table and say hello. They wear sparkly rocker T-shirts and leather arm cuffs, certainly too cool for Tijuana.

"Hey, can we buy you a drink?" one asks. "We just saw that stellar performance."

"Oh, thanks," Lani replies, blasé. "But I don't know if we need a drink, 'cause I just won all the Café Pacific tequila we can handle."

"Oh. Gotcha," she says. "We'd just rather sit with you girls than brave all these sleazy men alone, you know?"

"What do you think, doll?" Lani asks you.

The girls are tragically hip, but why the hell do they want to sit with you? On one hand they could definitely cramp your style—cut in on the attention you'll be receiving from the wet T-shirt fans. Then again, it might be cool to have more partners in crime. With these two on your side, you'd be causing bar brawls.

If you kind of wish you could join the hipster girl leather-arm-cuff gang, invite them to sit down and turn to page 74.

They're a little too Coyote Ugly for you. Blow them off and turn to page 207.

Pink is for girls! You decide that you are going to drink the straw-berry margarita and let your man drink the green . . .

You reach for the frothy pink glass and take a swig. It is sweet and powerfully alcoholic, but you don't taste anything out of the ordinary. "Well?" you ask Lani, "I chose. Did I get the button?"

"Somebody did," Lani says, smugly, "you're going to have to wait to find out who!"

You take another swig and look over toward Jesse, who cluelessly gulps down his margarita, peacefully oblivious. You've heard that Viagra takes some time to kick in if indeed it works at all, so you decide to sit back, relax, and enjoy your-self.

Your table is near a cool fountain in the middle of a beauti-ful plaza. It all looks more European that Tijuanan. A small mariachi band begins to play on the perimeter of the plaza, and dozens of buzzed tourists lounge at little tables, munching on chips and drinking ice-cold beers.

What a perfect afternoon. Not to mention Jesse keeps flirt-ing with you. He takes your hand and starts playing with your fingers, interlacing them between his, and tickling your wrist and the inside of your arm. You are in the middle of telling him how you won a beer-chugging contest in Chicago, when he places your hand on his knee and tells you earnestly, "You are the most exciting woman I could have ever hoped to meet." Wow. You look down at your hand resting in his lap, and then you see it. Jesse is growing the biggest boner you have ever seen. I mean, *massive*. He is pitching a tent, erecting the pyramids, raising the flagpole—he is sporting major wood. You are trying not to stare, but frankly, his penis is dangerously close to crawling out and attacking innocent bystanders. Make no mistake: Jesse has won "who's got the button."

You cautiously take your hand off his lap and place it on the back of his neck, trying to ignore his trouser snake. Playing with his shaggy hair, you decide that you cannot let an opportunity like this pass you by. You can't help wonder what it would be like to ride the snake, baby. "I want to get you alone," you whisper in his ear.

He nearly falls off his chair and stammers, "Yeah, um, definitely." He kind of fidgets nervously and asks, "Do you mind if I just run to the little boys' room? For one minute?" You tell him to hurry back. Jesse stands up, knocking several drinks off the table with his boner. You try not to giggle, but Lani unabashedly howls with laughter as Jesse scurries away.

Lani and Bill cackle like hyenas, obviously very pleased with the prank they played on poor Jesse. You just feel bad for the poor kid, getting drugged without his knowledge. He's such a nice and trusting guy. You look across the square, where Jesse has stopped to speak to a very fat and disheveled looking Mexican woman. See, that's what you're talking about! He's a humanitarian trying to help this poor old toothless lady who's probably hungry or has lost a child or something. Your heart melts as he takes the old woman's pudgy hand. He's probably giving her money.

But Jesse moves the woman's hand to his waist, leans in to

her, and kisses her full on the lips! Before you can scream, "Nooo!" Jesse is in a full embrace, making out with an old woman who is undoubtedly suffering from scurvy. You are shocked, appalled, and suddenly struck with more self-esteem issues than you ever had in your awkward pre-teen years. What does she have that you don't have? Tapeworms? Jesse and the massive woman leave the marketplace arm in arm.

You point out the disgusting spectacle to Lani. "Look!" you yell incoherently. "*You* did this! Pill—evil blue pill! Your fault— it was *you*!" But Lani's not listening, she's in her own Viagra trance, sucking face with chain-smoking Bill. This is like the Twilight Zone! Icky Bill? Action must be taken!

You find your purse and cigarettes, grab Lani by the hair, and try to un-suction her from Bill's nicotine-tinted lips. "Lani, look at me!" you yell, trying to talk some sense into her. "You are making out with a guy who is wearing *sweatpants*! We are leaving!"

"My God," Lani says, noticing Bill's attire, the blue pill haze momentarily lifted, "what have I done?"

The End

You're such a softy. You hand over five bucks to buy some gum from the kids.

The cutest little girl in the world happily hands you a huge box of Chicklets. *"Gracias! Gracias! Gracias!"* the kids shout, your new best friends. Lani is so charmed by their reaction, she hands over five bucks too. She almost looks a little misty-eyed as one little boy kisses her on the cheek.

"Kids. Gotta love 'em," she says wistfully. "So, what illegal shit are we gonna buy and bring home?"

"I read this article about how senior citizens come here to buy cheap prescription drugs," you say, offhand. "You don't even need a doctor's note. I bet they have Vicodin."

"Do I look like a former child star?"

"Prozac?"

"Lowers your sex drive."

"Valium."

"I'll just go through my stepmom's medicine cabinet and get them for free."

"Or there's always . . . Viagra."

"Now you're talking," Lani says with a look of pure excitement. "The little blue pill of wonder."

Both of you are now standing in front of a huge store with the words *"Farmacia"* blazed across the front. Inside, a gaggle of old folks give their orders in annoyed Spanish to the men behind the counter. In the window, you see a sign: Claritin on sale today only!

"Shit. They have Claritin! That's my drug of choice!"

"What are you talking about?" Lani asks.

"I have allergies like you wouldn't believe," you confess. "That shit's expensive, but it's the only drug that works and still lets me drink."

"I guess I understand. If you can't drink, what's the point of being healthy?"

"Damn right," you say, looking in your wallet. If you spend your shopping budget on Claritin, you can save a ton of money in the long run. You can finally afford to go out partying every weekend of the year and get Sapphire and tonics instead of the no-brand gin. You can even feed your car the good gasoline, or go to Victoria's Secret and finally update your sadly waning bra and panties drawer. You'll never have to be embarrassed on a second date again.

"Women can take Viagra, too," Lani says, her eyes glazed over in anticipation. It's like one of those cartoons where eyeballs become dollar signs, only Lani's eyes are becoming little blue Viagra pills. "It makes you crazy. Like multiple, multiple orgasms. With the power of Viagra, anybody can reach new dimensions." Lani walks into the *farmacia*, like a moth to a flame. She whispers something to the guy behind the counter, who shouts back a price. Lani checks her purse and looks to you. "I need to borrow some money."

You begin to panic. She needs money? You need all the cash in your wallet to buy your Claritin. A cold sweat begins. So many drugs. So many drugs! "Lani," you whisper, "what about my Claritin?"

"But . . . I really need this," Lani pleads, jonesing like a junkie. "Just one prescription, man . . . I swear, this is the last time. If you were a friend, you would help me out."

If the blue pill of destiny calls to you with its siren song, turn to page 51.

If the blue pill of destiny calls to you with its siren song, turn to page 51.

Enjoy your sex without additives and preservatives and save some big bucks on allergy medicine by going to page 84.

Enjoy your sex without additives and preservatives and save some big bucks on allergy medicine by going to page 84.

You would never pass up the opportunity to flirt with a swarm of hot men while under the influence of tequila. You grab Homer the piñata and hang with the hotties . . .

At the boys' table, you are greeted with high fives and exuberant applause from these adoring fans. Apparently they loved your "flash"-dance routine. Before long, your newest admirers are pouring you glasses of sangria and lighting up Dunhill cigarettes. Classy. You instantly forget the names of the hunks the moment they introduce themselves.

"Is it alright if I just call you all 'Trey' or 'Gorgeous' or something?" you ask. "It will make life much easier."

"Sure, sweetheart," one of the Treys replies. "As long as we can call you 'Dorothy.' How is that?"

"Keep buying pitchers, you can call me anything you want, Gorgeous." God you are good.

"Hey," one of the Treys asks, "are those the new Prada sandals you're wearing?"

"Yeah," you answer in shock. He must have been checking out your legs.

Another Trey proposes, "Would you ladies like to dance?"

You are the diva of the moment, so you might as well hightail it to the dance floor. Grooving together in a circle, you realize these guys are exceptionally good dancers, like Ricky Martin good. You're dancing in the middle of the circle, with the boys chanting "Surrender, Dorothy!" as you do your whole Madonna "Vogue" routine. One particularly hot Trey spins you around wildly, lifts you up, and tosses you around like those Olympic ice dancers. You can't remember ever having this much fun dancing in your life. That is, except for your little routine an hour ago on stage. As the music slows, you wrap yourself around Cutest Trey and nuzzle his chest. God, he smells so good! You tilt your head up and place little kisses on his neck. He jerks back suddenly and pushes you away.

"Um, I'll be right back. Promise," he mutters, marching off the dance floor. Mortified, you wonder what his deal is. Does he have a girlfriend or something? You notice all the other Treys are speaking to each other very closely, like they are conspiring or something. What the hell is happening? You find a similarly dejected-looking Lani across the dance floor.

"What is *up* with these guys?" you ask.

"I think they're flirting," Lani replies. "And *not* with us."

The light goes on. "Oh! I get it! They're gay!"

"Bingo."

"Then why the hell did they pick us up?" you ask, sneaking off the dance floor.

"We," Lani says, "are cock-blockers. You know, fag hags. Just our luck."

"I'm so lame!" you whisper. "I tried to kiss one of them! I practically *attacked* him!"

You walk back to the table and pick up Homer while Lani pockets the Dunhills and grabs the pitcher of sangria and two cups. "I know a place where these ladies can't find us," Lani says, marching you into the ladies' room. You take a seat on the bathroom counter and pour yourself a drink. You clink glasses.

"Surrender, Dorothy," you toast.

"Surrender, Dorothy."

The End

You earned that donkey drinking your ass off, and no nation's border is going to separate you!

"Sorry Señor," you tell the rancher, "this burro is not for sale." The man sighs and walks away, shaking his head. You look at Daisy and for a moment you're sure he understands the decision you just made. Then he gets distracted by a potato-chip bag on the ground and swallows it.

"Well, shit." Lani says, "I reckon I've never smuggled an animal across the border before. How are we going to pull this one off?"

"I don't know," you say, lighting a Parliament and throwing one to Daisy, "it's not like we can hide him, or pretend he's anything *but* a donkey."

"Oh my God, that gives me a great idea," Lani grins.

Thirty minutes later, you approach the border with Daisy in tow. You and Lani wear homemade "Animal Rescue" T-shirts. You've draped Daisy in a giant Mexican flag that reads: "Found in back of Taco Bell. I was almost your dinner." The crowd parts, people in line gasp and let you through, chattering and taking photos as you cut to the front of the line at the border checkpoint.

A haggard old lady in a border-patrol uniform approaches. She looks like the type who has seen it all. She lets out a little chuckle and looks Daisy up and down. Lani clears her throat and tries to sound political. "We are members of People for the Ethical Treatment of Animals."

"Yeah, as in PETA," you pipe in. Lani gives you a withering look of death.

"We rescued this animal from a local eating establishment and we are taking him to a shelter in the States."

The border-bitch looks skeptical. Someone behind you takes a photo of the animal. A crowd of tourists has formed on either side of the border crossing. Another flashbulb snaps. Lani whispers to the lady, "I don't think you want to be on the front page of the paper as the woman who condemned a donkey to a future as taco meat."

The woman takes out a rubber glove. Snapping it onto her hand, she expertly shoves her arm into Daisy's most intimate spot. "Standard procedure," the woman explains. Daisy neighs in shock. You and Lani gasp in horror. Daisy is not a virgin anymore. After the woman finishes her rectal probe, she peels off the glove, and waves you through.

Daisy's skittish for a few days after her border-patrol molestation, but after a few buckets of oats, carrots, and Parliaments, he works his way through the trauma. Unfortunately, it only takes you one week to discover that you can't live with a donkey in your apartment. When Daisy gobbles down an entire bottle of Dexatrim and doesn't stop shitting for three straight days, you know he has to be in a more welcoming and tolerant environment, and you know just the folks to adopt him.

At the local Phi Delta Theta fraternity, Daisy eats like a prince, always gets treated to cigarettes, and even has his own troth of keg beer. He lives in a large yard, where he munches grass while fratboys play Frisbee and barbeque around him. At night, he is a hit at the parties, usually wearing a sombrero or a Phi-Delt baseball cap. Every so often, you visit him, feed him Parliaments, and pet his snout. You know Daisy loves living the swinging bachelor life. And when you look into his eyes, you know taking that last kamikaze shot was the right thing to do.

The End

***One hot Latin guy doesn't get to cramp your style! Jump on stage
and start grooving!***

You blow the Latin Lover a kiss and swish toward the stage.
The club staffer boosts you and Lani onto the stage, and the
crowd erupts into applause. The DJ cues up a great song, and
Lani twirls her hair and shakes her ass at the audience. You follow her by bumping, grinding, and pretending you are going
to flash the crowd.

As you shake your moneymaker, you scan for hot men. The
hottest of all is the Latin Lover, who stares at you intently. You
wink at him and subtly turn away to give him a view of your
fabulous ass. He's approaching the stage closely now, Corona
in hand. How nice, you think, he bought you a beer. But before
you can understand what is happening, he puts his thumb over
the bottleneck opening, shakes the beer furiously, and sprays
you. You are so shocked you can only stand there, slack-jawed
and soaking. Lani shrieks as some other piggish man has
joined in, spraying her as well. Before you know it, you are the
center of a full-fledged beer assault; dozens of laughing men
hosing you down with their brews, expecting some sort of
shower show dance routine. Your hair now matted to your
face, you grab hold of Lani and awkwardly hop off the stage.
By some miracle, you manage to get back to your table and
grab your belongings.

"Oh, fuck me," you whisper to Lani, "get me out of this
place in one piece. If any of these assholes try to touch me . . ."

Heading to the front door means a trip through ass-grab-alley, a maze of tables where lecherous men sit and taunt innocent young women. The faces of the leering perverts loom in front of you.

"I've got it under control," Lani says. She grabs two beers off a cocktail waitress's tray and hands you one. You take a swig, and look at her quizzically. She puts her thumb over the bottle opening, and shakes the beer while approaching the ass-grabbers.

Just as you are in range, a fat hairy man yells: "Hey bitches, I'll dry you off!"

He may as well have declared war. Lani turns in slow motion, gets the rude asshole in her crosshairs, and sprays him directly in the face. You join in, giving these guys a taste of their own medicine. The fat pervert and his friends have been silenced.

"Anybody else want a piece of me? Huh?" you scream at the pervs.

The ass-grabbers suddenly look meek, and you take the moment to run to the front door and burst into the glaring bright daylight. Lani runs into the street and hails the first taxi-cab. You climb into the car, and your ass squishes and sloshes against the bench seat in back. "It's going to be a long, sticky ride home," you say, lighting up a smoke.

The End

You could never tear yourself away from an episode of **The Love Boat**—*and you are not about to pass up an opportunity to get on board an actual love cruise!*

"We are in! Lani, darling," you shriek, giddily hopping up and down in your chair, "we're taking to the high seas, beee-yatch!" Lani groggily comes up for air from macking on Jaws and nods drunkenly. Affirmative! At this point, you could tell her you're all going on a camel ride and she would agree.

Outside the club in the blinding sunshine, the Guys escort you into a massive black sport-utility vehicle. Inside, you're impressed to see it has its own mini-bar and TV sets. You and Lani kick it in the backseat and open cold beers, while the men play video games. "Ugh," you say to Lani, "I can't stand those games. Really, it's so immature."

"Look," she says, "there had to be something wrong with them. But hell, they have fancy cars, a freakin' yacht, and they know how to treat two goddesses like us. I'll let them sneak in a round of Tetris." She has a point.

You arrive at the dock, and walk toward a monolithic boat. The thing is massive, glittering, and several stories high. Printed on the side of the bow is the boat's moniker, *The Snowman*. You step on board and you're greeted by a wood-paneled lobby and a goddamn chandelier. As far as you can tell, there is also a formal dining room with a 360-degree view, a master bedroom with a vibrating bed, and bathrooms with those eight-headed showers. On the front deck is a full bar with a bartender, and a hot tub! You spend the first fifteen minutes on the boat running around giddily with Lani like it's Christmas morning. Talk about "pimped-out"! By the time you make it back to the Guys, the boat's sailing out to sea. You wrap your arms around Guy and marvel at the open ocean.

You spend the afternoon swimming, hot-tubbing, tanning, drinking, and eating fish caught directly off the boat. "Guy," you say, "you should be careful about spoiling me like this. I could get used to it." He leans over and kisses you sweetly. Hmmm. The perfect moment is interrupted by Lani, who yells for more Parliaments. "Fine, fine," you say, heading inside in search of cigarettes. In the dining room, you spot Jaws and three other Guys around a table. You stop dead in your tracks when you see what's on the dining room table: an impossibly huge, *Scarface*-style pile of cocaine. You are freaked out.

"Um, excuse me," you politely interrupt. The Guys look up from sorting the powder into little baggies, "I am assuming that's not confectioners' sugar and you are not making Christmas cookies."

"What, you want a bump?" one of the Guys asks. You're not sure if that's sex or coke, but right now you're pretty sure you don't want either.

"Sorry, but isn't this all a little 1980s?" you joke, nervously.

"Hey," says Jaws, "what's wrong with the '80s?"

"Nothing," you reply. "The '80s were great. I was really into stickers and the training wheels came off my bike! Jesus, don't you think this is just a little excessive?" you indicate the mountain of drugs, "I mean, who are you, Belushi and friends?"

"Look, angel," Jaws says, "We're doing a quick little deal in

Ensenada. A no-brainer. If you want to come along, we will cut you and your friend in. Bringing ladies along on the deal is a sign of good faith. You and your friend could earn twenty thou and you don't even have to get off the boat. Just keep your mouths shut and come along for the ride."

"And what if I decide to just say no?"

"There's a popular surfing spot not far from here. We can drop you off, and I'm sure you can catch a ride back into TJ from there." Jaws flashes his toothy grin. "But seriously babe, you should hang with us."

Your judgment has been severely affected by the alcohol, and the snowy mountain of blow transfixes you. One thing keeps reverberating through your head. Twenty thousand dollars. Twenty thousand dollars.

If you can pretend to forget how **Scarface, Boogie Nights,** *and* **Goodfellas** *ended, play coke slut for a day and make some dough by turning to page 61.*

You would rather take your chance on a beach full of surfers than a boat full of cokers. Turn to page 166.

You cannot risk Daisy being violated by the border patrol. You have decided to sell him to the rancher.

"Okay," you sigh. The man smiles, and begins to count off several bills. You pet Daisy on the snout, and feed him one final Parliament. "Good-bye," you say softly, "Be good now, and make lots of good farm friends. I'll miss you." Lani takes the cash from the man, and unloads your shopping bags from Daisy's back. You slowly untie the rope from your wrist, and hand it over to the rancher. You place a little kiss on Daisy's head, gulp back a sob, and say, "Good-bye, boy."

The man walks away, and you turn to Lani. She hands you the cash with a heavy heart. Feeling terrible, you watch the rancher lead Daisy away. In the distance, he takes off his rancher jacket, and throws it onto the donkey's back. You see the back of his T-shirt has writing on it. You strain to read: "XXX Dirty Donkey Revue."

You gasp in horror and your knees buckle. It's a terrible realization that will take years to get over. You've just sold Daisy into prostitution.

The End

Those fratboys with the video camera can find their entertainment elsewhere. Your vomit is your own business, and you'll be open for business any second now.

You let go of Lani's hand and bolt into the public toilet, which is really nothing more than a metal shack. You slam the door in the face of the fratty asshole with his daddy's video camera, and let your eyes adjust to the darkness of the tiny room. There—you spot it—a hole in the ground with a flat tire for a "seat"—not like you're gonna sit. You bend down, afraid to let your knees touch the ground. The horrific smell hits you and it doesn't take much for your stomach to understand this is it.

What happens next is not pretty: Your guts rebel against you, and with one horrendous retch, you vomit out any and all contents of your stomach. It disappears into the hole, and you swear between retches that you hear rats scurrying down there. Die vermin, you think, as you cough out the last of whatever's left.

"Oh, God," you sigh, exhausted. How do those girls with eating disorders do it? There is nothing grosser than this *Exorcist* routine. At least you can breathe normally again. A paper napkin, a breath mint, and you'll be back on your feet in no time. You've learned your lesson; it's bottled water from now on.

"You okay in there?" you hear Lani ask from outside.

"Much better," you say as you head for the door you slammed only moments before. You try the handle. No handle. You look for the lock. No lock.

"Planning on spending the day in there?" Lani asks, her voice a little worried.

"I think I'm trapped," you say, slamming your body against the heavy door. It won't budge. You look up to tiny slivers of light streaming in. Lani tries to open it from the outside and you keep pounding, but it's pointless. This place is a steel trap and you're caught inside. Claustrophobia has never been a problem for you, but here in this smelly box, you feel terribly anxious. As your eyes fully adjust to the darkness, you can see the steam rising from the abyss where your lunch just went. The day is only going to get warmer.

"I'll be right back!" Lani says.

"Don't leave me!" you scream, but it's too late. You're panicking now, shouting, "Somebody help *me*!" but nobody does. That scurrying you heard earlier hasn't gone away. In fact, it's getting louder. Guess where you're spending the rest of your Tijuana experience? Trapped in a fetid, stinking rathole.

The End

There is no way you are going to drown in this guy's saliva. Give him a sloppy kiss good-bye.

"Not today, Diego," you tell him. You pet his cheek, a heartfelt farewell. This is all met with a look of confusion.

"But wait!" he says, eyes pleading. "You will regret this."

"Hey, 'no' is the same in English and Spanish," you inform him. "I'm leaving now to find my friend." You turn to go, but Diego grabs your wrist firmly. He suddenly looks drunk and menacing.

"I am not going to let you go," he grumbles.

Okaaaayyy. This calls for harsher tactics. You lean in to him and say, "Fine. I will go upstairs with you, but first I have to go to the ladies' room." He seems unsatisfied with your answer. You rush over to the table, where Lani entertains two teenage boys, and grab your purse. "Bail out, bail out!" you whisper to her, motioning to Diego. "Meet me outside in two minutes." Lani nods, understanding. You try to avoid him on your way to the bathroom, but he's relentless, shadowing you so closely you're surprised he doesn't follow you into the girls room and try to hold your hand while you pee.

Once inside, you donate your breath mints to a pair of vomiting drunk girls and make your way to the back of the bathroom. In the last stall, a window about the size of a doggie door opens into the adjacent alley. You've climbed out of much trickier windows before; this should be a piece of cake. You strap your purse around you, tie back your hair, and climb onto the toilet seat. There is a knock on the door. Diego's voice calls out, "Are you all right in there?"

"I'm fine," you yell back, "just a minute!" You push the window out, and hoist yourself up. There is only a four-foot drop into the alley, so you squirm your way slowly through the tiny window, trying to maintain your balance. You manage to get your hips through, and suddenly you pitch forward, the world flips upside down, and you smack your head with a solid thud. Yeeowch. You slowly rise from a crumpled heap, amazed to be alive. It doesn't feel like any bones are broken, the only damage is a ripped skirt and—oh shit—a huge gash has opened up along the side of your leg.

Lani pokes her head around the corner, and runs toward you. When she sees the wound, she screams bloody murder. The last thing you remember before passing out is being lifted by two teenage boys wearing shirts that say "Horndog Drinking Team." Then black.

You wake up in a room with two parakeets, a cage full of roosters, an iguana, and three orange kittens in a cardboard box. Lani bursts through a door and gives you a big hug. "Oh my God," she blubbers. "I am so glad you are okay! We thought you were in a *coma* or something!"

You look down at your leg and see that your battle wound has been stitched up with plastic blue thread. "What is this?" you ask her.

"Oh," Lani says, helping you to your feet, "it's all the vet could find."

"What? A vet? As in veterinarian? You took me to a zoo doctor and he sewed me up with fishing line?"

Lani shrugs. "Any port in a storm, baby."

You hobble through the doors, and out onto the street, where the guys in "Horndog Drinking Team" T-shirts wait for you. Lani introduces you to your rescuers.

"How are you feeling?" one of the Horndogs asks.

You rub your aching head and try to smile. "I feel like a hundred bucks."

"So now what?" Lani asks, shoving a Parliament in your mouth.

You take a drag, thinking for a moment. "Well," you say, "dancing is out for me . . . but I could really use a stiff drink."

For the rest of your life, people will ask you how you got the scar on your leg. Although the story has been exaggerated over the years, the bottom line is this: You had one hell of an adventure in Tijuana and you have the scars to prove it.

The End

You have decided to spend your hard-earned cash on yourself—not a table full of pretty boys! Start your engines, you are going shopping!

"Let's get out of here," you say, grabbing the Homer piñata. "Sorry champ," you say to the handsome American. He looks too good to be true—which means he's probably gay.

Bursting out of Café Pacific and into the bright daylight, you recoil like a vampire. The heat is thick and all the smells of the city hit you solidly in the face. Walking toward the market-place with Homer under your arm, you wonder what to buy in Tijuana. A donkey? A woven blanket? A woven blanket that can be draped over a donkey? This is not the fabulous shopping that Lani promised.

"Lani, we just turned down seven gorgeous men. I'm doing the math here—that's nearly one thousand pounds of hunky man flesh."

"Combined, that's about forty-two inches of dick we will never be enjoying," Lani says with a sigh. "But I think I have an idea that may take the sting off our newfound celibacy."

You find yourselves at a typical pharmacy with rows of aspirin, Band-Aids, and the like. Lani heads to the young man who works the counter at the back of the store. *"Hola,"* she says, flashing him a brilliant smile, "we are Americans. Can you help me with something?"

"Anything I can do for you, I will." He answers in perfect English.

"Anything?" Lani asks in a conspiratorial tone. Lani turns to you, "Well, you're the big winner today, what do you want to buy?" You stare at her blankly. "Drugs! You know, anything you want."

You smile and turn to the young man and ask, *"Hablas Ganja?"*

"Meet me in the alley behind the store in ten minutes," he says with a wink.

"Oh Christ, is he serious?" you ask Lani. "I never would've said anything, but I'm so wasted! Wasted enough to try to buy *weed* out of a pharmacy!"

"Look. Compared to what they usually sell out of the back of pharmacies, it's nothing." Lani shoves a cigarette in your mouth and says, "We have ten minutes to kill in the market-place. Then it's weed time."

As you wait for the minutes to tick by, you check out the lame stuff they're hocking on the streets: sombrero ashtrays, Barney the Dinosaur piggy banks, and T-shirts that say humorous things like "Got tequila?" And then a glistening in the corner of your eye catches your attention. You are inexplicably drawn to a stand in a far corner of the market. A dazzling and brilliant light hypnotizes you. It's overwhelming, overpowering. Angels sing and the clouds part . . . for you have just reached a state of nirvana. Here before you lies a stand full of Judith Lieber knock-off purses, hundreds of them, each one completely covered in rhinestones.

"Hallelujah!" you breathe.

"Thank you Lord for this bounty," Lani whispers.

They have purses that look like roses, pigs, ships, boxes of

Chinese take-out, lipsticks, frogs, and (you are weak with excitement) shoes, each one swathed in brightly colored crystals! Each one is a piece of art—and then—ohhhhhhh . . .

"Lani, look! It's a Diet Coke can!" you shriek as you hold up a purse that looks like a life-size can of Diet Coke covered in rhinestones. "If I don't own this, I will regret it the rest of my life."

"They have one that's a Corona bottle!"

"Lani, we *need* this."

"But what about the weed?"

You realize that sacrifices will need to be made. If only you could have a rhinestone purse full of weed, then life would be so sweet! But God works in funny ways. Will you spend your hard-earned striptease cash on illegal drugs or on so-tacky-they're-cute purses? Better hurry, you don't want to miss your back-alley appointment.

If you can convince yourself a Diet Coke handbag is something you would actually use (I mean, what doesn't match red and white?) turn to page 159.

Or if you'd rather have the kind of bag that is green, sticky, and smokeable, get thee to a dark alley and turn to page 39.

*You came here for one thing—***action.** *So go get some.*

"Let's go upstairs," you whisper in Diego's ear. He grabs your hand and escorts you off the dance floor. You walk by your table where Lani entertains two impossibly young-looking men. You wink at Lani and signal that you are heading upstairs with your new man. Lani holds up her camera and snaps a candid photo of you and Diego. At least if you black out, you'll have proof this guy was real.

You ascend to the third floor of the club, which overlooks the dance floor. With the exception of the DJ who smokes a spliff in his booth, the coast is clear. Diego leads you to a large dark booth in the corner, motions you to sit down, then slides up next to you and kisses your neck. Ugh, slobber. You pray you won't get a hickey; you would never live it down. Thankfully, he starts kissing further and further down your chest, over your shirt, and toward your belly. He stops to swirl his tongue around the rim of your belly button. You shudder in disgust, but he looks up at you smiling and says, "Yes, you like?"

You hate to break his heart, so you nod weakly. Besides, he is getting close to giving you serious oral pleasure, so what if he makes a pit stop or two on the way? Diego kisses your waist and moves toward your crotch, kissing all the way. He is moving lower, and you reposition your hips and subtly spread your legs a bit. Lower, and lower, until he kisses your thighs, and the tops of your knees, then your calves. What the fuck is going on? He missed the money spot! Diego expertly removes your shoes, and sucks on your big toe. It's kind of gross, sticky, kinky, and hmmm . . . after that long walk across the border, you figure you may as well enjoy the footbath. You lean back and let Diego run his tongue in between your toes, across the arch of your feet, swirl around your ankles. Well, this is a new experience. Sighing deeply, you reach for the Corona on the table and take a long swig.

Flash!

Suddenly, a bright light blinds you. Then you hear the unmistakable cackle of Lani's laugh! She has caught you—and forever documented the oral pleasuring of your feet!

Back in the States, months later, you will not remember much of your Tijuana adventure, but you will have a photo that could ruin your political career. In it, you're lounging back with your skirt hiked up, swilling a beer with a Mexican man sucking off your toes. That was definitely a Kodak moment.

The End

The crystal Diet Coke purse has a trancelike power over you. It must be yours.

"Lani, let's do it," you say, pulling out your winnings. "My treat."

"You totally don't have to," she says, petting her jeweled Corona bottle purse, "but we will be bonded in sisterhood for the rest of our lives if you do."

"Done!" You walk up to the saleswoman and pay for both purses. You're so excited, you don't even haggle for a better price. Just as the transaction is complete, a row of hanging ponchos suddenly rustles behind you. You spin around to see the lens of a large video camera! A man with a microphone pops out of nowhere and addresses the camera.

"As you can see, they come from the north," he reports to the camera, "in search of good times and good bargains. In Tijuana, however, things are not always as they seem. I am standing here at a popular handbag booth in a typical market-place. This woman has just purchased these little trinkets to bring home to the States." The camera zooms in on you as you stare back, frozen with confusion. "Miss, will you please hold up your new purse so the folks back home can see?"

You dumbly show them your Diet Coke rhinestone purse.

"And what did you pay for that little gem?"

A microphone is thrust into your face. "Forty-five dollars."

"This young woman has no concept of the true price of this mere bauble," he says to the camera, "a price paid of child labor and human bondage."

The reporter leads you to a large van parked nearby, camera following close behind you. The woman who sold you the purse is raving in Spanish, unable to stop the adamant reporter. He rips open the back door of the van, revealing a dozen emaciated children, all holding little jeweled purses in their tiny hands. You gasp in horror and disbelief. It's a mobile sweatshop.

"Conditions like these are all too common," he addresses the camera once again, "children forced to work fifteen hours a day, in such environments, often denied the basic needs of food, shelter, and clean toilet facilities. They are beaten if they try to escape, prisoners of an industry that depends on the greed of ignorant American tourists." The camera turns toward you. The reporter thrusts his microphone in your face and asks, "now that we have uncovered the dreadful truth of these conditions, what do you have to say for yourself?"

You take a deep breath. "Does this mean I have to give my purse back?"

The End

Puking in public is unacceptable unless, of course, you're on MTV getting paid for it or something.

You lift up the final shot, and the crowd falls silent. You then pass it over to Lani who swiftly shoots it down. The mob moans and groans but thankfully disperses in search of other crude forms of entertainment. The Ghostbuster boogies away to find other gullible young women, so you and Lani light up more ciggies in an attempt to quell your churning stomachs.

"I never thought I would say this today, but I could really use a glass of water," you say, sloppily trying to balance your head on your hands.

Lani looks at you in horror, and says, "Don't even joke about that. The water here is lethal." Lani stands up, grabs you by the wrist. "The only way to ride this buzz is to work it through. No water. We are dancing it off!"

She drags you onto the rotating dance floor. The second you hop on, the world starts spinning and your equilibrium shifts. You slowly work your way to the center of the dancing mob and start doing your best hip-swishing and rump-shaking. A Prince classic starts to pump, and you and Lani do a "Diamond and Pearl" pseudo-lesbian routine. You grind Lani from behind, while she pretends to spank your bottom, the two of you swishing your hair around like glam-rockers.

A thin man taps you on the shoulder. He wears a "Le Machine" T-shirt, clearly part of the club staff. For a second, you're sure he is going to eject you and Lani from the club for lewd behavior, but instead he motions for you to climb up a large cubelike platform, a miniature stage. Wow, you have always been a bit of an exhibitionist, but to graduate to this? You and Lani can be two drunken girls grinding on top of a riser. It's too *Showgirls*—too crude, too raunchy, too . . . fabulous. You are strangely drawn to the concept. As a matter of fact, you feel unnaturally compelled to dance on the giant cube.

You march toward the cube with a sense of urgency, but before you get there, a strapping Latin gentlemen intercepts you. You pause to give him a drunken once-over. He is what you would call a tall drink of water: large and muscular, dark skin, black eyes, and long dark hair tied back into a ponytail. Dressed in black from head to foot, he looks swashbuckling, cheesy, and totally Antonio. You give him your most coquettish smile and say, "So Zorro, where's your sword?"

"Wait and see," he whispers thickly in your ear.

Your heart drops and your knees buckle. This man is smoking hot. Should you sacrifice your stardom and stay with this mysterious Latin Lover? But maybe your exhibitionist nature is too strong and can conquer your raging hormones.

You did not travel all this way to NOT have a Latin love affair—turn to page 88.

Who needs a man mucking up your good time? This is ladies' night! Start shaking it onstage and turn to page 143.

You've convinced yourself that the Taco Bandito's homegrown tequila is probably the Mexican version of a microbrew. And screw it, you're thirsty.

You lunge for the greasy bottle, ignoring the crud imbedded in the cork top as you lift the bathtub tequila to your lips. The first sip is tasteless, whatever devil's spice he put in the taco acts as a buffer between your taste buds and the tequila. Then you take a huge gulp, and the burning in your mouth begins to subside.

"Are you okay?" Lani asks.

You nod, smiling, and bring the bottle up for another drink. The sweet añejo and whatever the hell else is in tequila has fermented to perfection. It's a golden gift from the cactus gods. You could drink this straight for hours and never need a chaser. It's the best tequila you've ever tasted. The Taco Bandito grins at you through his not-so-fresh teeth.

"You like?"

"This is *muy bien!*" you try to say in your grade school Spanish.

"I make myself. At *mi casa*. From family recipe." He produces a rolled goatskin from nowhere. On it, in Spanish, is a list of complicated directions and ingredients. It's withered and worn with age, a treasure map to tequila magic.

"What would it take for me to buy that from you?"

"Oooh. I don't theeenk so," the Bandito laughs.

Lani laughs with him, shooting you a look that asks, Are-you-off-your-fucking-rocker? You hand her the bottle. She sniffs it, reluctant, then takes a sip of the tequila. After a moment, she looks at you with new respect.

"This is amazing tequila," she whispers.

The Taco Bandito's eyes get misty, and he speaks like he is very far away: "This recipe was won in a blood duel between a wealthy baron and my great-great-great granpapa. The baron killed my great-great-great granmama for this tequila and will forever suffer for it. The recipe is all that is left of her."

"Oh. Wow. Blood duel?"

"Which is why it is very expensive."

You surprise yourself and make an offer right then and there. "I've got about a thousand in the bank. A hundred on me. Is that enough? That's everything I have."

"*Si, señorita.* For that, I give you family recipe. For that, you will be worthy to carry on tradition."

"Dude, blood duel tequila is the best!" Lani looks like she has seen God. "We'll go into the booze business full time!" Flashing forward five years, you dream you have the newest hottest tequila on the market. And, when the cash starts rolling in, you'll buy the Taco Bandito a Rolls Royce, or a house, or the biggest taco stand in Tijuana! All you need is that recipe and everything will be set! Of course, the rational side of your brain is beginning to talk. Give this guy all the money you have? You can't chuck everything for the tequila-queen dream, because that's what it is, a dream, not reality. This whole blood duel thing could be the greatest line a local ever gave a tourist to empty a bank account.

Do you want to take every penny you have and buy the Taco Bandito's homegrown tequila recipe? If you think so, turn to page 79.

Your taste buds are out of whack and your brain's fuzzy. There are a lot of things you can do with that money that don't involve a blood duel, so move on and turn to page 169.

You get paranoid smoking weed in your own apartment. There is no way you can handle the shadiness of a cocaine deal.

"Okay, Falcon and the Snowman, I want off this drug boat. And pronto." Jaws and his buddies look disappointed, but it seems like they understand. You leave them to their mountain of cocaine. After you pack up your stuff, you tell Lani about the drugs and inform her that the two of you will be making an early debarkation.

The boat slows down, pulling closer to the shore. Guy motions toward the shore and says, "Adios, ladies." About two hundred yards away is a gorgeous tropical beach, littered with tan bodies lounging in the sun. The surf breaks right beyond the boat, and young men on longboards coast on wave crests back to the shore. "This is it," Guy says, pointing over the edge of the yacht, "now get off."

"What?" You ask, stunned. "You just want us to get off *here*? We could drown!"

"Just so you know," says Lani, "I really don't swim outside of hot tubs."

"Maybe I am not making myself clear," Guy snarls, "Start paddling, bitch." And he seemed like such a nice guy, that Guy. You grab Lani by the hand and walk to the edge of the boat. You are in the middle of gauging how long it would take to swim when you see a young, tan, blonde man rowing a sea kayak beyond the surf! He could bring you in!

"I will handle this," Lani says, and pulls up her shirt, flashing the kayaking man. As expected, he instantly turns his kayak back toward you and pulls up alongside the boat. Lani puts on her most flirtatious smile. "You might get lucky if you can give us a ride back to shore," she tries shamelessly.

"Sure thing, ladies!" the kayak man says, your knight in shining armor.

You drop your bags into the back of the kayak, bid the Guys good-bye, and try to gracefully climb down the yacht's ladder. Your kayak man, whose name is Shane, helps you into his boat, giving up his seat and swimming next to the kayak like some bronzed sea king. As you crash through the surf toward the shore, you don't miss the Guys at all. You hit the beach and feel like kissing the sand, you're so thankful to be on solid land. Shane drags his kayak up the shore, and invites you to come and have a cold beer with some "brahs" down the beach. Frankly, nothing sounds better.

As the sun dips into the ocean you sit on the sand around a campfire with the three hot, yet scruffy looking guys. They all wear woven hemp ponchos and board shorts, talking in surfer slang. You and Lani tell an exaggerated version of the coke-boat story, and by the time you are finished, the surfers believe you were held at gunpoint and made to walk the plank before Shane valiantly saved you. Lani has even taken up a game of footsie with Shane, her experience with Jaws but a memory.

One of the surfers gets up and says he has to "get stateside to see my big mama." You jump up and brush the sand away and ask for a ride back into Tijuana. He says it's "cool." As you gather your things, Lani runs up to you and pleads, "Can't we stay a little longer? I am having such a great time here . . ." You glance over at

Shane and know what her real intentions are—she wants to do a *From Here to Eternity* bit with tangled bodies in the crashing surf.

"Hey," one of the surfers says, "If you want to stay I've got some primo ganja." Now you are really annoyed. You have to get back to Tijuana and Lani's car sometime, don't you?

"Listen, *brah*," you say sarcastically, "I'm sure your stuff is the 'diggity dank' or whatever, but we really need to be going." He shrugs and pulls out the baggie of weed. You catch your breath. Holy shit—it's furry and purple, like something out of a *High Times* "Bud of the Month" spread. You have never seen anything like it before! Suddenly intrigued, you sit next to the surfer to examine it.

"Um, I'm going now," says the guy on his way to "big mama." You are torn. You could very easily stay here and smoke, lie on the beach, and just chill, man. But will you ever get back? You don't even know where you are . . .

How can you pass up an opportunity to smoke the Bud of the Month? Turn to page 113.

Isn't smoking dope on the beach the way that girl gets eaten in Jaws? Hitch a ride back to TJ and turn to page 111.

Tequila may be a powerful elixir, but there is no way you're going to let it dictate your life path. You'll keep your cash and your pathetic bank account and move on.

Lani pays the guy five American dollars for the rest of the bottle, so she's happy, but you'd just like to forget about it, the stuff probably wouldn't pass whatever FDA requirements there are to legally sell booze anyway. Yet, you can't escape that nagging feeling that something has passed you by and that there is now a hole in your life.

"There's a hole in my life," you explain to Lani as she swigs from the bottle.

"You're drunk. Drunks always think there's a hole in their life, so they fill it with more booze. Here," Lani offers you her bottle.

"No thanks."

The two of you wander the streets, ducking into shops and looking at sombreros with witty phrases on them. Nothing cheers you up. Even when Lani shows you a statue of a monkey surfing, you can't bring yourself to smile. All you see around you are desolate streets, people trying to feed their families, drunken tourists (you're *so* not like them), and a lost goat. What had started off as a brilliant vacation retreat has turned into a dull, smelly afternoon.

"Ohmigod! Freeze-dried frogs!" Lani exclaims, barreling into a shop. In the window are a bunch of real frogs, long dead, stuffed and shellacked in place. They wear small sombreros and have been posed to look like they are in a mariachi band. It makes you sad. You're about to burst into tears when you hear it . . .

Bark!

You look around. That almost sounded like a dog barking. It was more like—

Bark!

Behind the ponchos, past the freeze-dried frogs, in a corner, there is a small box. You look inside and instantly smile. There, smiling up at you, is a litter of the cutest Chihuahuas you have ever seen. One gets up on his tiny paws to look you in the eyes. He is black, with brown markings that make him look like the world's tiniest Doberman. He looks at you with his big animated eyes and wiggles his batlike ears. There was a hole in your life, but no longer.

"Pepe," you say, smiling like a mother who sees her baby for the first time after all the goo has been cleaned off of it. You and Pepe are soulmates.

Outside the store, Lani rushes out, excited. "Look, I bought the frog mariachi band! I'm a goddess!"

"I bought a dog," you say, showing her Pepe, cradled in your arms. "I'd like to take him home."

Back in the states, six months later, you're living the charmed life. Lani calls it "The Luck of the Chihuahua." There's a guy who you met at the dog park that may be *the one,* and even Pepe loves him, so you know it has to be fate.

One night in the shower, you're doing some extreme acrobatics to shave your legs. While cursing men everywhere and the American standard of beauty, you suddenly lose your balance. *Whap!* You're on your back, lying on the shower floor, in excruciating pain. You've thrown out your back and hit your head pretty hard. Everything hurts.

"Oh, shit," you moan. Panic sets in. Who knows you're here? Nobody. Your boy is home visiting his folks, your neighbors are selfish assholes who would never think to check on you, and Lani isn't coming over to see you for three days, when you're supposed to watch *Sex and the City* together. You're going to die. Your life was going great, and now, like some old retiree whose body won't be found for weeks, you've fallen and can't get up.

Bark!

"Pepe?" you manage. Pepe noses his little face into the bathroom. He sees you, and instantly understands the situation. Your vision's fading. That smack on the head must have been worse than you thought.

Bark!

"Pepe . . . call . . . nine-one-one," you tell him. Pepe looks at you, confused, his little Chihuahua mind trying to comprehend what you're saying. "Pepe . . . *nueve-uno-uno* . . ."

Pepe's big ears immediately perk up. He prances to your phone in the hallway, knocking it off the cradle. You're fading fast, but before you black out you swear the last thing you can see is Pepe's little paws pressing those magic numbers. Nine, one, one.

When you wake up in a hospital, Lani, your boyfriend, and a dozen of your closest friends are at your side. The biggest story in the country is how Pepe saved your life. Letterman's calling and wants you both on for "Stupid Pet Tricks." The Humane Society has given Pepe a medal that weighs as much as he does, and the folks at Purina have awarded you both a lifetime supply of dog food.

"I am so glad we went to Mexico," you tell Lani. Pepe hops into your arms and begins to lick your face with puppy love. *"Gracias* Pepe . . . *gracias."*

The End

You once drank beer that had been buried in the woods. Admit it, there is not much you wouldn't do for booze . . .

"You've got yourself a cocktail waitress," you say, picking up two of the massive glasses. Shit, these are heavy, you think. You tell yourself that this is your upper body workout for the day. You finally arrive at the booth and set down the load.

"Todd, you pussy!" One of the men yells at Mr. Teeth, "I cannot believe you made these beautiful ladies do your grunt work, fuckface." He extends his hand to you and says, "I'm Guy." Guy is a perfect name for him; it reminds you of your childhood pet, a cat named "Cat." Guy is straight-up tall, dark, and handsome. He introduces you to all his buddies as he moves over to let you slide in beside him. You shake hands with Tims, Jims, and other men whose names you are destined to forget.

"You know what?" you say to the table, "I am just going to call *you* Guy," you point to Guy, "and the rest of you 'another Guy,' okay? It's just easier that way." The men look at you, amused, "Except you," you point at Mr. Teeth, who is drinking from a huge cup with the shark toy sticking out of it. "I'll call you Jaws."

"And what should we call you?" another Guy asks.

"You can call me whatever you want, as long as you're buying." The group of Guys laugh. God, you are so *on* right now! As you sip one of the massive buckets of booze, you get to know the Guys. Turns out they are all in business together in San Diego, some sort of brokerage crap that sounds like a real snore. They're down in Mexico for a *golf* vacation, which is also dubious in your mind. But they sure know how to treat a lady. They constantly offer you drinks that they mix from their own little mini bar, and the second you whip out a cigarette, three lighters are in your face, offering to spark you. You even tell Guy about the dude who called you "prime orgy material."

"That is so inappropriate," he says, dead serious. "I apologize for my gender. Do you want me to kick his ass?" You tell him that you appreciate the offer, and will keep it in mind.

Hours later, you are buzzing along, half-shitfaced, and not intending to slow down. It's impossible to calculate how many drinks you have had, but it's somewhere north of seven. Across the booth, Lani is making out with Jaws, and Guy is giving you a backrub.

"You should join us this afternoon," Guy whispers in your ear, "on the yacht." Did you hear that right? The Yacht? "It's docked here, and we were going to go on a ride, have a party, have some food, go swimming. Sound like fun?"

Maybe it's just the gallons of tequila talking, but it does sound like fun. Sunshine, yachts, parties, yachts, food, yachts . . . You cannot believe that you have gone this long in life *without* yachts. Then again, on the water, no one can hear you scream. Is that safe? I mean, there's a thin line between acting wild and acting stupid, and that line gets harder to see by the moment. Maybe you should look for it at the bottom of your eighth margarita . . .

Miss Adventure #1

You have always fancied yourself a sea-faring, yachting kind of chick. Ahoy matey, go on the boat ride and turn to page 145.

You prefer to be on dry land when you party with complete strangers. Stay ashore and turn to page 64.

Throw that cute fish back in the sea! This is supposed to be girl bonding after all!

"Listen, Backstreet," you say, gazing into his eyes, "I am going to have to cut you loose." He looks disappointed. You pinch his cheek and say, "I have a feeling you will get lucky before the day is through." He gives you a high five (who does that anymore?) and kisses you on the cheek.

You find Lani, who announces that she has to "break the seal" as she heads for the ladies' room. You are left alone for a while, and use the moment to reapply some lip-gloss. A very short, twenty-something guy comes up to you and says, "So, kid, what's the good word?"

"Word?" you answer. "Excuse me?"

"You know," he snaps at you, "what's the deal? What's going on? What's the word?"

"Are you trying to ask me to dance or something?"

"Look," he says, "I see you sitting here alone, with no one to talk to. I'm trying to do you a favor here."

"Thanks," you say sarcastically. What is up with this guy? After taking a seat next to you without permission, he automatically grabs one of the cigarettes off the table and starts puffing away.

"I'm Glen," he starts, "I'm here with some buddies for a bachelor party. On our way to Ensenada. Private estate, that kind of thing." He looks at you to see if you're impressed yet. Chatterbox Glen continues, "Down here from L.A.—did I mention I was a producer?"

Shocker.

"Look," you interrupt, "I am just waiting for my friend. She's in the ladies' room, I'm sure she will be back soon. It's been nice meeting you." He doesn't catch the hint. Are you going to have to spell it out for him? Are you going to have to sew him a quilt that says "Fuck Off"?

"Kiddo," he snaps, "your friend's not coming back. Take a look." You scan the club and see Lani across the dance floor doing her typical sultry dance routine . . . with Backstreet! This is the guy you just cut loose because this was a "girl bonding" trip! Now you are stuck here with some obnoxious dwarf who won't shut up. Glen puts his arm around your shoulder and says, "Kid, I want you to come with us. A dozen of us are going to another club down the street. Let your friend have some privacy."

You look at Lani cuddling up with Backstreet and gulp. You are in a very fragile, emotional, and drunken state right now. You either feel like crying or entering a tequila-drinking contest. And then there's Glen. You hate to admit he's right, but you might have a good time with a dozen men at a bachelor party. Sure, you don't know them, but it's better than watching your best friend make out with your discarded boy-toy!

"Take it or leave it, sweetheart," Glen says, pulling the cigarette from your mouth and snuffing it out, "we're on a schedule here. Time is money."

*If you would rather sit alone like a loser, watching Lani's **Showgirls** act, turn to page 181.*

Twelve-to-one odds are pretty good. If you would rather be the lucky lady at the bachelor party, turn to page 48.

You are not going to be taken advantage of and ripped off by a few corrupt and arrogant police officers! It's time someone stood up to them!

"Pardon me," you say, brushing aside the policeman, "I am going to go inside and file a report." As you cruise by the men and into the police station you add, "and I am sure your supervisor will not be happy to know that not only are you gambling on the job, but you're soliciting bribes from young women." You strut through the station's front door.

As the station door slams shut behind you, you notice that there is absolutely no one behind any of the desks in the front room, no one behind the counter to the left, and no one in the tiny jail cell area to your right. "Huh," you say to Lani, "I bet everyone is just on siesta or something." Lani does not offer any support, as she's too busy petting her air freshener like it's a kitten.

"Lani, I've got it," you proclaim. A brilliant idea has come to you with the power of a thunderbolt. You put all your shopping bags down on the front counter and start riffling through your purse for your cell phone, "I am going to call AAA and see if they can help us. I bet you there is some sort of service that can file a report or something." You ring 411 information, throwing Lani a quick wink. She cracks a meek and hopeful smile, which vanishes as the police officer and his gambling cronies walk into the station. The main officer approaches you, looking unhappy. You tell him, "I'll be right with you, I'm on a very important call." You huff and turn away, doing your best to ignore them. But for some reason he doesn't leave. He's breathing down your neck, standing right behind you.

"Is this yours?" the officer casually asks, pointing at your shopping bags. You nod yes, distractedly. Before you can protest, the officer reaches into one of the bags and pulls out the M-80 explosives. He screams in Spanish so loud that you drop your phone. Suddenly all the craps-playing officers surround you with guns drawn. You put your hands up. Lani does the same. Her evergreen air freshener flutters listlessly to the ground.

Before you can say "miscarriage of justice," you're cuffed, dragged to the jail cell, and locked inside. How can they do this to you? What are they locking you up for? "Hello!" You yell at the officers outside the jail cell, "*Hola!* Why are you locking us in?" The main police officer saunters over to your cell with the shopping bag of M-80s.

"These are very dangerous. You might have been trying to blow up our police station." He grins and starts to chuckle through his gold-capped teeth. Lani stares off at nothing, having her own private breakdown. You're going to have to take control of this situation.

"Aren't we allowed a phone call?"

He takes a telephone off one of the desks nearby and hands it to you through the bars. Trembling, you take the receiver and begin to place a telephone call that you have hoped you would never have to make. As you hear the phone ringing on the other end of the line, your stomach churns in dread. Little tears start to well up in the corners of your eyes, and your throat tightens.

"Hello?" a woman's voice answers the call.

You take a deep breath. "Hi, Mom? I'm in jail . . ."

The End

You figure that if you go with Glen, Lani will eventually steal him anyway. You would rather wallow in drunken pity alone.

"Glen, I am going to have to take a pass on this one," you say. "I'm a loner. A rebel."

"Loner, yes," he says standing up. He is as tall as he was sitting down. "Rebel, I doubt it."

"Fuck off, short stack."

Glen is too shocked to answer and storms away red-faced. You light up your last cigarette and try not to look toward Lani and Backstreet. You take a healthy drag and give yourself a pep talk: This is the best time of your life. You are free, young, sexy, and independent. You should feel great! When else in history could a single woman sit alone in Mexico slowly getting wasted during the daytime?

The music in the club starts to slow down and it's some Faith Hill song that you have heard in airport lounges and Kleenex commercials. You listen to the twangy, crappy love song about how she can feel her lover breathing, and then it hits you like a ton of bricks . . . Oh God, you are *alone*! Alone in this miserable shit-hole club with no one's breathing to feel! You take a slug of beer to try to suppress the drunken tears that are coming now. For a moment you consider tracking down Glen, the dwarfy chatterbox, but now he is gone, too! And he could have been the one, if you weren't so quick to judge. Staring into your empty pack of cigarettes, you drunkenly cry at how cursed your life is.

The End

You know when you have stayed too long at a party. Time to get the hell out of Dodge.

"On the count of three," you whisper in Lani's ear, "run." She nods and you glance over toward Señor Bookie. He is not looking. "One," you say under your breath. "Two." Lani takes a drag of her smoke. "Three!"

You dash out of the party and into the street, pumping your legs and arms as hard as you can, hoping that no one noticed your escape. It's tremendously hard to run in heels, but you manage, clomping noisily with every footfall. Lani keeps stride next to you, fleeing down the street but still smoking her cigarette. God bless her, you think.

"Can you believe," Lani says, between huffs and puffs of her cigarette, "people actually like to do this for *fun?*" You're within eyesight of the center of town and slow to a walk, gasping for air. For the first time since you ditched the party, you check behind you.

"Lani?" you ask, "Is that what I think it is?" The bookie is a few blocks away, with a posse of six or seven men. They almost look like one of those angry mobs in the movies with torches and hounds. They've set their sights on you, coming closer and closer at an alarming speed.

"The car! It's our only chance!" Lani shrieks. You both run like hell, darting through the mazelike marketplace, knocking over baskets, rugs, and small children. The debris you have scattered behind you may slow the mob, but it's gathering more members—all the people whose merchandise you've just wrecked. You turn to say something to Lani, but she's gone! You backtrack to find her standing at a booth full of rhinestone purses.

"Aren't they the most fabulous things?" she says, holding up a sparkling purse in the shape of a frog.

"We have to blow this taco stand, like, *now!*" you scream, yanking her away from the purses. You gotta admit it was a really cute purse, but there's time for shopping and right now it's time for escaping an angry mob. You can see Lani's hot rod a few yards in front of you now. Almost there. You look back over your shoulder and see the mob is about four blocks away. You rule! You have plenty of time, you're definitely gonna make it.

Once you reach the car, you tug at the door. Lani digs in her purse, frantic. "Where the fuck are my keys?" she shrieks. The men are closer now, and Lani's found her sunglasses, cigarettes, stolen shot glasses, but not her car keys.

The bookie and his mob, sensing your helplessness, stalk toward you menacingly. You huddle next to Lani, hoping your bitchy stare will scare them away. No such luck. One of them brings out a switchblade. Oh God, you think, this is where you get stabbed and bleed to death in a dirt field. The guy with the knife walks toward you, running his tongue along his rotting teeth.

You take your last breath and close your eyes, suddenly very religious as you say silent prayers to God, Jesus, Buddha, and anyone else you can think to pray to. But nothing happens. Reluctantly, you open your eyes. Where did the guy with the knife go? Did your prayers work? The knife-wielding guy and his cronies are crouched in the dirt, working on Lani's car tires. Señor Bookie and his banditos have pried the hubcaps off her car! After that, they make quick work of the side mirrors, windshield wipers, and front and rear bumpers. Their speed and efficiency is quite impressive—in a matter of thirty seconds, the entire car has been stripped. They don't even say thank you as they run off laughing, bumpers and hubcaps under their arms.

Lani stands in awe, gawking at her bare car. "My poor car!" she cries, "It's naked!"

You can only smile sheepishly and say, "I guess I should have bet on black."

The End

You throw the old "you are what you eat" notion out the window. Buckling under the peer pressure, you have decided to eat the worm.

"Eat the worm! Eat the worm!"

You lift the shot glass off the table and take a deep breath. You give one last look at your slimy little friend and bid it a silent apology before closing your eyes, throwing the shot back, and quickly swallowing. When you open your eyes, dozens of shocked faces stare back at you. Suddenly, everyone in the club bursts into applause!

"Wooo Hooo!" you shriek with excitement. Lani stares at you in wonder. "Get in my belly!" You scream, rallying the crowd.

"Wow. I worship you. You are my personal hero," Lani sighs, lighting your menthol.

"Thanks, G." You're chasing that worm with beer, figuring it's best to wash away whatever bacteria it carried. Smoking your menthol, you notice that the tip of your cigarette makes really neat designs if you swirl it around. Whenever you drag on the ciggie, an orange streak floats out behind it. Soon you're making figure eights, circles, and waves, even spelling out words, like "worm."

"Oh my God, you are totally tripping, aren't you?" Lani asks, breaking up your little game. "What does this look like?" She waves her fingers in goofy patterns in front of your face.

"Do it again!" you beg, between uncontrollable laughing fits. "Make the pretty rainbow, Lani, please!"

"Listen," Lani grabs your shoulders and talks to you in a very serious tone, "You are having some sort of hallucination. You need to relax, okay?" Her serious demeanor just makes you giggle even harder. "Hey! Listen!" She yells. "I am going to try to find you some water, okay?"

"Water in Spanish is agua, agua, that's a fun word. Agua, agua, agua, agua." Lani shakes her head and leaves, unable to grasp your profound realization.

Someone taps you on the shoulder and you spin around to see a familiar face. It is Dan, your old friend from high school! "Dan," you ask, "is that you?"

"Wow, I thought that was you," he says, "But everyone here calls you 'the worm-eater,' so I wasn't sure. You actually ate it?"

"Yes," you answer, "and thank God you are here 'cause I'm seeing tracers everywhere. It's like an acid trip."

He laughs at you and takes a slug of beer. Maybe it's just the worm, but you think that Dan has gotten mighty fine looking. Why didn't you hook up with him in high school? He turns to you and all of a sudden you are filled with a lusty wave. Just on cue, Lani runs up to the table with an armload of bottled water. She pops the top off one of them, hands it to you, and says, "Not one word out of you until you finish the bottle."

You obey and start chugging the cold water. Mmmmm, agua feels good . . . When you finally come up for air, you notice that Lani is packing up all your stuff and paying the bill. "We're leaving?" you ask.

"I think you need some air, honey."

You look at Dan, and he says, "I was thinking we could dance awhile."

Lani looks at you like you are about to have an alien baby. "Whatever you want," she says. Maybe Lani's right. You probably could use some air . . .

Try to resist the hallucinations, stay at the club, and try to mack on your old buddy. Turn to page 193.

You would rather trip outside, dude. You need to roam. Turn to page 200, man.

Okay, you're having flashbacks to those babysitting years. Kids looking up at you with pleading eyes? Forget it. You're not that weak.

"No!" you shout, a little louder than you wanted to. One of the youngest kids gasps, his cute little pudgy cheeks trembling with rejection. Tears well up. You feel like utter crap.

"Oooh. Look—ceramic monkeys," Lani says, dragging you away. She has never had a problem saying no to people. It's amazing, you think, she'd probably make a really great loan officer.

"I can't think of anything I need more in life than a ceramic monkey," you say.

"Follow me. I saw a guy walking out of this store with a kick-ass surfing one." Lani says, leading you down a dank alleyway. At the end of the alley, there is a rusted door that looks like it hasn't been opened for years. The stench of urine is almost as bad as it was in your ex-boyfriend's bathroom.

"I think we're the only monkeys down here."

"Yeah . . ." Lani says, looking nervous. The two of you head for daylight, stepping over bodies of dead cats. At least you hope they are cats. Then—a shadow passes over the two of you. Three huge men are blocking the exit to the street. You squint to see their faces. The smallest of the three huge men has a face criss-crossed with scars, the middle one has only one tooth, and the big boy Papa Bear looks slightly retarded and still angry about it. These are the Three Not-Your Amigos.

"Oh *shit*," you whisper. You're trapped. Near the entrance

to the alleyway, you see the gang of Chicklet children passing by. They see what's going on and pause to watch, like rubber-necking at a freeway accident. "Hey kids—remember us? We need help—" The little kid who you made cry just points at you and laughs. The Chicklet children run off, cracking up. Note to self: you are *never* having kids.

"*Hola*, ladies," Scarface says with a grin. His boys are on you so quick it's like you barely have time to fight back. Papa Bear rips your purse out of your hands. Lani yelps as Toothless grabs her adorable little purse and flashes her a gummy grin.

"Hey dickweed!" you shout, sounding rather badass, "You can have our cash and our phones and our motherfucking Tic Tacs, but you don't need to keep our passports."

"You can keep mine, the picture sucks," Lani mutters, defeated. You shoot her a glare. "Or *not*, because we need to get home," Lani tries. Scarface whispers to his thugs. Papa Bear grabs Lani by the wrist, pulling her close to him. Lani has gone pale with fear.

"Just so you know, I have a raging case of herpes," Lani tries.

"Me, too," says Papa Bear.

"Okay lady," Scarface hisses. "We make a deal. You can have one passport now and one passport after. Once you help us get this through to the United States," Scarface says. From a bag, he brings out a ceramic monkey. It actually has a smiling face and sits on a surfboard. How charming.

"You want me to smuggle that into the United States?"

"A man will be waiting for you. You give him the monkey, he makes a phone call to us, and we let your friend go."

"What if we say no and tell you guys to fuck off?"

"Then, good luck getting back home."

You are hating this trip already. This is totally bad karma for not having bought gum from the Chicklet children. If you try and smuggle the monkey across the border, you could end up getting thrown in jail. You've seen *that* movie before and it never ends well. But these guys even have your calling cards and change purse, so there's no way to get home.

"What are we gonna do?" Lani asks you, terrified.

Maybe a nice girl like you will get across the border without question. With NAFTA and people way weirder than you trying to get into the United States, it should be a breeze, so turn to page 36.

This whole scenario is not worth the risk. Find another way to get back to the land of the free and the home of the brave by turning to page 42.

You think the white rooster is just plain cute. You are going to bet on him to beat up that old cranky black one.

"Blanco," you say, pointing at the round white bird. The Señor with the money pouch nods his head, makes a note on a scrap of paper, and saunters off.

Lani looks perplexed as you return to the party. "Why did you pick the dumb-looking fat one?" she asks.

"Someone has to take a chance on the dumb white guy, and it's usually me," you lament. "Besides, it's twenty dollars. Who cares?"

Minutes later, the crowd starts chanting and pushing to get up to the stage. People scream for this or that chicken, waving money around in clenched fists. You drunkenly stagger closer to the stage to get a better look. What you see next is probably not dissimilar to one of those pornographic crush films, where naked women in stilettos crush rats to death underfoot. You see the black rooster kicking the flesh of the severely wounded white bird, repeatedly burying the spikes on his feet into his fleshy side. Whitey is not even putting up a fight, and eventually he staggers to the ground and lies down, streams of blood staining his white feathers. Whitey is now fajita meat.

You toast to the demise of Whitey at the bar a few moments later, and Señor Bookie approaches you. He says something to you in Spanish, which you obviously don't understand at all. You and Lani continue to drink in hopes he will go away. He persists.

Finally you hold up your hands and say loudly, as if he is hard of hearing, "I don't understand a fucking word you are saying." Now *he* looks annoyed. What is this guy's problem? The man pulls out a piece of paper and writes down "20." You shrug and say, "Yes, I already gave you twenty dollars." He circles the "20" and then writes out "300." What the fuck is this, some sort of fucking puzzle? You are about to ask Lani how to say "fuck off" in Spanish when she whispers in your ear.

"He wants more money, because your rooster lost."

"Fuck that!" you slur drunkenly.

Lani holds up her hands and tells the man, *"Un momento, señor."* She pulls you to the other side of the bar and begins, "Look, we are drunk, single, American women in a party full of rowdy cockfighting fans and we owe them money, *comprende?*" You nod slowly. The situation dawns on you. You are fucked. "We really don't have many choices," she continues, "we can make a run for it. Or we can stay and give them everything we have. The choice is yours."

Why do you always have to make life-altering choices in a tequila haze? You look around at the men at the party. You could definitely outrun them; most of them look like they've been eating pork rinds and lard their entire lives. On the other hand, everyone has been kind to you so far, so perhaps you can just throw them a couple packs of cigarettes and they'll leave you alone.

You are too drunk to even think about running in heels. If you decide to face the music and reason with the cock mongers, turn to page 77.

You have always wanted to make a literal run for the border. Run as fast as you can and turn to page 182.

You are a slave to your hormones, you perv! Go ahead and give Dan a whirl on the dance floor.

"I want to stay," you say.

"Okay, trippy," she answers, probably too weirded-out to argue with you. "But no more worm for you. Only agua from now on." You nod and open a second bottle of water.

Dan leads you by the hand onto the dance floor. The two of you start grooving to some old funk tunes, and soon you are practically inseparable. With the residual effects of the tainted worm, the lights swirling above the dance floor look amazing. You wrap your arms around Dan's shoulders and know you've never felt such a soft shirt in all your life. The whole experience turns totally groovy, dude. There is really no such thing as a slow song in a Tijuana club, so people just cling to each other and make out during all the songs. That will be the two of you any moment now . . .

"Let me ask you something," Dan says, tickling the back of your neck, "were you this cute in high school?"

"I get cuter every day," you answer, inches away.

"You know something, I believe that." When you lean in and kiss him, it's a transformative experience. The endorphin rush mixed with the toxic worm sends you to new sensual heights. You continue to kiss for what seems like a very long time, but who knows, as your whole space-time continuum is out of whack.

When you finally make your way up from his embrace, you look around to see that Lani, sitting back at the table, has also found a companion, who seems to be teaching her how to blow smoke rings. "That's my friend, Monkey," Dan whispers in your ear. "They seem to be getting along. The two of us are driving down and spending the night on the beach in Rosarito. You should both come."

"Whatyoutalkingabout, Willis?" you ask

"If we don't go soon, we are going to lose our room." He is giving you a wink. "Nice suite, too." Rosarito? You don't even know where that *is*. And, although attractive, do you really want to ditch out with High School Dan? What about the car? What are you even supposed to be doing tomorrow? Plus, you are tripping on a hallucinogenic worm, so can you truly make an informed decision?

And then you look at Dan. Yum.

Want to spend the night with an old friend in a foreign city while you are tripping on a magic worm? Be our guest, and turn to page 197.

If you would rather stay put and ride out your trip in TJ, turn to page 200.

In roulette and cockfighting, you always bet on black. It's practically your motto!

"Negro," you say, pointing to the black rooster.

Back at the party, you decide it's time to kick it up, and move from the cervezas to the tequila. You and Lani spend a few minutes discussing what the black rooster's name should be. You both settle on Tyson. (You are especially proud of this double entendre of a black fighter and poultry.)

The mariachi trumpeter blazes out a note and all attention is turned to a giant chicken-wire arena. The two cocks are brought out in their cages. A man holds the white bird high above his head and the crowd roars. "Boo!" you yell, "down with whitey!" Then another man holds the black bird high, and you scream, "Go Tyson! Mama said knock you out!" The crowd presses toward the stage. You can't see much, but do you really want to watch two hopped-up birds kick each other to death?

You and Lani toast to Tyson and take a tequila shot. Suddenly, the birds are let into the arena, and the crowd starts clamoring. Over the shoulders of the men in front, you can see feathers flying in the air. The birds are making a terrible squawking noise, and you swear, you just saw an entire bloody white wing fly out of the ring. Suddenly, the crowd is jumping, cheering, and hugging each other. One of the men onstage reaches into the ring and holds up the bloody carcass of the white chicken. You and Lani are jumping up and down squealing hysterically at Tyson's victory.

You park yourselves at the bar, and eventually the Señor with the money pouch approaches. He hands you a *huge* stack of foreign money. The bills are colorful and the numbers are outrageous. You have never seen so many zeros in your life. "Oh my God, Lani," you say, fanning out the money like a lotto winner, "we are millionaires!"

"Let's turn this into greenbacks, baby!" Lani shouts, ecstatic. You skip out of the party toward the center of town and find a tiny currency exchange kiosk. After waiting in line for 20 minutes and coming dangerously close to losing your buzz, you finally approach the teller at the window. You hand him the stack of bills and request dollars. He counts the pesos, calculates, and hands you back . . . four dollars.

"What?" you shriek, "this is not right! I gave you millions of pesos!"

"Ahh," the banker replies, "those were the old pesos, not the new pesos." You are stunned and confused. Four dollars doesn't even buy a pack of cigarettes anymore.

"Come on big spender," Lani laughs, "let's go blow this on a pack of Chicklets."

The End

One road trip isn't enough for today? Buckle up, you are going south!

Within half an hour of making out on the dance floor of a seedy club, you are hurtling down a Mexican highway with your future husband du jour. Lani is a few miles behind you in her hot rod, riding down with Monkey, who is supposedly "playing navigator." You wonder what other games they're playing; they seemed pretty cozy.

Dan blares his CD player while he steers his Jeep through the hills south of Tijuana. You have unrolled the window, sticking your head out in the warm wind like a dog. You're finally starting to feel somewhat normal again. Now that you are no longer in a drugged-out haze, you're surprisingly happy to be on this impromptu trip. It's a true adventure, cutting through this barren deserted land. There's not a soul in sight. It's roadrunner country.

You finish your fourth bottle of water, and start to feel uncomfortable. You really should have peed before you left, but it was too confusing; deciding to go, getting to various cars, getting directions and cell phone numbers, all while tripping balls. Now you're in the middle of nowhere with at least four bottles of water in your bladder, along with dozens of tequila-laden drinks.

"Um," you say awkwardly, "I know this isn't an opportune time, but I need a pit stop."

"Yeah? How bad?"

"Like, DEFCON two."

"Wow. Okay, well, it looks like you're going to have to kick it the way nature intended. Pee outside."

He's right and you're desperate. This is a glamorous turn of events. Make out with a hot guy, then squat in a desert and pee in front of him. Super. Dan pulls the Jeep over on a dusty embankment on the side of the highway.

You hate to admit it, but this is not the first time you have had to pee al fresco. Experience dictates that the best technique is to squat and lean back while holding onto the bumper of the car. This gets you close to the ground and keeps your shoes out of the splash zone. Cursing your small bladder, you hike up your skirt, pull down your panties, and take a deep breath. You are peeing. And peeing. Good Christ what did you drink? You're creating a new river in this barren desert! What seems like two full minutes later, you hear the unmistakable sounds of a car approaching. Moving fast, you put yourself together as the car pulls over behind you. For a moment, you're certain it's Lani and Monkey, probably trying to take a photo of you bare-assed to the world. But, no. Oh, much worse. It's the *Federales*. You scramble back into the car as two "police officers" approach.

You sit petrified in your seat. Dan whispers, "Fuck me," pulling out his wallet. One of the *Federales* knocks on the driver-side window and gives the international signal for "roll down your window, you fucking gringo." Dan does.

The officer speaks to him in Spanish, and much to your surprise, Dan *answers* him in flawless Spanish! But they still seem to be having a heated exchange. You're encouraged that you haven't heard anything that sounds like it might be the word for "prison" or "ass-rape."

Dan finally turns to you and says, "He is not happy about you urinating in a national forest area. They want one hundred American dollars to let us go. I have about twenty—can you cover it?"

You do have eighty dollars, but it would clean you out. Then what? What if things didn't work out with Dan? Would you end up stranded and broke in Mexico, selling tortillas out of a shack for the rest of your life? And can they really blackmail you like this? I mean isn't it against the law?

If you decide to trust Dan and bribe a police officer with your cash, turn to page 203.

If you would rather try to handle this the way normal law-abiding citizens would, and keep your pocket money, turn to page 86.

You would rather ride the snake outside, man.

You burst into the harsh, hot sunlight and your heightened senses are overcome by the smell of dust and urine, the blazing heat that makes the air look wavy, the sounds of sputtering trucks and a mariachi band playing in the distance . . . Again, it could be the trippy worm, but everything seems so garishly beautiful, you want to write poetry about it all. Beside you, Lani stomps out a cigarette on the pavement.

"I want to go to where that music is," you say to her excitedly.

Lani perks up her ears to listen to the mariachi music, and then shakes her head. "No," she says, "that music's coming from the residential side of town. It's probably some kid's birthday party or something."

But the sounds of the guitars and trumpets mesmerize you. "No!" You say more adamantly. "I really want to see. The music is calling me." You can tell Lani does not trust your judgment, but thinks it would be unwise to disagree with you in your current hallucinatory state.

You glide through the residential neighborhood, snapping your fingers like little castanets to the music, which grows clearer with each little shanty you pass. About four blocks down, you come to an empty residential lot—and it looks like a block party is underway. Dozens of locals dance boisterously, and a mariachi band plays on rickety risers being used as a stage. In the midst of the party are a makeshift barbeque and a table that glistens with bottles of tequila and icy cold beer.

Lani smiles at you and asks, "Feel like crashing a party?" As if she needed to ask! Two Pacificos later, you and Lani are kicking up your heels with the rest of the party, dancing to the mariachi. So far, the only song you recognize is "La Bamba," which must be the national anthem of Mexico. The men and women are incredibly friendly, and grab you and Lani and spin you around to the music.

A man circulates through the crowd with a small sack, and people hand him wads of money. He works his way toward you and Lani. "I think he is taking up a collection for the beer," you say.

"All I have is a fifty." Lani says. You look at her like she is speaking Greek. Who the hell carries fifties? The man approaches you, and you pull your last twenty out of your purse and hand it over. The man looks shocked and grateful. You smile demurely. Certainly these people could use it more than you. Besides, you have had such a lovely time . . .

"*Negro? Blanco?*" the man asks you.

"*No, gracias.*" You answer, unsure of what he is asking.

"*Negro? Blanco?*" He asks again. You turn to Lani and she shrugs. You are at a loss. Finally, the man gestures with his hand for you to follow him. He leads you toward the stage.

"What is this all about?" Lani asks.

"I have no idea. I think he is trying to say thank you or something. I did give him twenty American dollars." The man leads you to two large cages sitting on the ground. In one sits a huge white rooster. In another sits a black rooster. He indicates each, "*Blanco*" and "*Negro*."

"No thanks," you say, "I don't need a chicken. But thank you so much for your hospitality, it's really great . . ."

"No, you idiot," Lani cuts you off. "He wants you to *bet* on one of them. They are fighting roosters." Looking closer, you see that the white rooster has a sharp razor blade fastened to one of his feet. The black rooster has a spiked spurlike weapon strapped to his leg. You gasp. It's like fucking *Gladiator* or something. This is hideous, you think, where are we, in ancient Rome? This is supposed to be a civilized country!

"Do I have to?" you plead, but you are getting the feeling that this Señor is not returning your dough. You look at the white rooster, then the black one. Okay, you are no expert at this, but here goes: The white one is fatter, so that means what? He is slower but harder to kill cause he has so much fat? The black one is taller, which would help in basketball, but in cockfighting, who knows? The black one also looks meaner, but older. Mean, good for cockfighting, old, probably not. As you are comparing these two prizefighters, Lani is rolling her eyes and the man is getting impatient. Time to decide . . .

"Don't trust whitey" couldn't be all true. Take your chances with white and turn to page 191.

"Always bet on black" is your favorite Wesley Snipes line, so turn to page 195.

You have heard too many horror stories about Mexican jail. You figure this could be the best eighty bucks you will ever spend.

"Alright," you grumble, as you pull out your wallet. "This is the single most expensive piss I have ever taken." Dan hands the money to the officer, who has the gall to count it before putting it in his pocket. What kind of a country is this?

Then, just when you think it's time to hit the road again, you hear a rapping on the window next to you. You turn to see the second officer, who is also giving you the "roll down, you fucking gringo" sign. Oh my God. Does he want money too? You're both fresh out! You unroll the window and he begins arguing with Dan in Spanish. This time, Dan seems really upset. This could be bad.

Finally, Dan looks at you and says, "He wants something from you."

"But I don't have any more cash, and neither do you!"

"That's not what he wants." You gulp and fear the worst. Perhaps you will be learning the Spanish word for "ass-rape" after all. "I am so sorry," Dan says, "but he wants your bra."

"My fucking bra?" you ask incredulously. "This is retarded. This is definitely not in the law code, I don't care how fucked up this country is." Taking off your bra might be an invitation to these assholes. You cross your arms and think: What bra did you wear today? Is it one of your boring ones? Can you buy another bra in this God-forsaken nation, or will you be free-falling the rest of the trip?

If you want your Victoria's Secret to be a secret no more, unfasten that bra, and turn to page 205.

This is sexual harassment, without a doubt. And so undignified! Keep your bra on and turn to page 86.

Would it be a real party unless you lost your bra? Make the poor bastard's day, and hand over your cups.

"I can't believe I am doing this . . ." you sigh, as you reach behind you to unfasten your bra. You slip it out the side of your sleeve, a Houdini-esque trick you learned in summer camp. You hand it over to the second police officer and mutter, "Tell your wife I say 'you're welcome!'" Your comment clearly confuses the officer, but once he lays eyes on your little lacy number, he starts to grin like a schoolboy who has discovered his dad's porno collection.

The *Federales* jump back in their car, and hang your bra around the rearview mirror. You kind of feel like a deer that's been shot and mounted in someone's den. You light a cigarette and try to regain some composure. "Men," you are mumbling, "the same in every country. Immature twits with dicks for brains . . ."

"Hey," Dan says, "thank you for that. You really saved our collective asses."

"Oh, you will repay me," you say, "in tequila and various sexual favors. I am going to make you earn it, make no mistake." Dan guns the Jeep, peeling off the shoulder and onto the highway. The site of the urination crime is far behind you. On the remaining ride south, you manage to hammer out an agreement with Dan, regarding payment for the loss of your bra. You have negotiated: one thirty-minute foot-rub, two decent packs of cigarettes, one hour of "anything" you want later in the hotel suite, plus all the margaritas and tacos you can cram down your throat. The only thing you have to promise him in return is that the next time you lose your underwear, he is the lucky recipient.

Two hours later, you are sitting on a terrace outside one of Rosarito Beach's premiere cultural centers, the Museum of Tequila. Who would have thought that your hotel would be adjacent to the largest collection of tequila in Central America? Around the table, you are animatedly telling the tale of how you narrowly escaped fascist and perverted police officers in the high desert. Monkey and Lani applaud as you raise your glass and say, "and that, my friends, is why I am not wearing a bra."

The End

There is no way you're sharing the spotlight with these ladies. Say no to the wild girls and hang with Lani.

Those girls keep staring at you all night, whispering and pointing in your direction. After a while, it gets irritating. Not to mention all the guys in the club are paying attention to them instead of you two. You'd think they were famous or something. That night, you and Lani drive back to the States, already hungover before the day ends.

A week later, Lani calls you and frantically yells at you to turn on the television and switch it to MTV.

"Oh . . . my . . . GOD!" you shout. There on television, are the girls you dissed at Café Pacific. They're hanging out and being interviewed with the one, the only . . .

"Madonna! Hellooo!" screams Lani.

"They were Madonna's backup singers and we totally dissed them."

"I could have been a dancer for Madonna! I missed the chance of a lifetime."

For the next ten years, every single time anybody even mentions Madonna's name, Lani goes on a tirade about how close she was to being one of her posse. After a while, it gets so irritating you won't even listen to her music. Your little jaunt to Tijuana did the one thing you never thought possible: It made you hate Madonna.

The End

Acknowledgments

Thank you to Amanda Patten, Sarah Self, and especially our agent, Paula Balzer, at Sarah Lazin Books. We'd also like to thank our family for all their support, and our friends for their inspiration and encouragement. Without you, this book would be a notion instead of a reality.

Beware

of lecherous hosts and backstabbing competitors if you want to be crowned the next Miss Liberty in...

Miss Adventures #2

Beauty Queen Blowout

by Lilla and Nora Zuckerman

COMING FROM FIRESIDE
SEPTEMBER 2003

FIRESIDE
A Division of Simon & Schuster
A VIACOM COMPANY